THE WOLF

THE WOLF

JOSEPH SMITH

JONATHAN CAPE

LONDON

Published by Jonathan Cape 2008

2 4 6 8 10 9 7 5 3 1

Design © Suzanne Dean
Illustrations © John Spencer

First published in Great Britain in 2008 by
Jonathan Cape
Random House, 20 Vauxhall Bridge Road,
London SW1V 2SA

www.rbooks.co.uk

Addresses for companies within The Random House Group Limited can be
found at: www.randomhouse.co.uk/offices.htm

The Random House Group Limited Reg. No. 954009

A CIP catalogue record for this book
is available from the British Library

ISBN 9780224085199

The Random House Group Limited supports The Forest Stewardship
Council (FSC), the leading international forest certification organisation. All our
titles that are printed on Greenpeace approved FSC certified paper carry the FSC logo.
Our paper procurement policy can be found at: www.rbooks.co.uk/environment

Typeset by Palimpsest Book Production Limited, Grangemouth, Stirlingshire

Printed and bound in Germany by GGP Media GmbH, Pößneck

For Louise and Clarke

CHAPTER I

From up ahead of me through the trees I can hear the sound of hooves crunching on snow. Everything else is silent. I stand with my breath clouding around my head in the cold air, not moving as I listen, not seeing anything except the white ground and the dark spiked tree trunks. I can smell the beast. Its scent is clean and strong and rises up from the cooler smells of the forest, enticing me, calling me towards it. It cannot be far away, but the trees grow so thickly here that I cannot see it and so I move forwards, walking with delicate steps between the trees, skipping over fallen branches, all so quietly that only a mouse sleeping in its burrow beneath where my paws land might open an eye, to close it a moment later as I pass.

Over the sound of the beast's hooves comes a snort, short and loud and in this silent forest like thunder. It must be large, this one, as my pointed ears not only hear the sound that breath made from the beast's nostrils, but from where it began, deep in a wide chest from big powerful lungs. I move forwards a little quicker. It may have snorted to clear its nostrils because it senses danger. The wind is in my favour and it will not have smelled me yet, and though I am still moving as silently as the gentle wind itself, these beasts have powers I do not understand. If it thinks it is in danger the hunt may well be over before it has begun.

I move through the trees listening to the regular thump and crunch of hooves on snow, my heart beating a little faster, my nostrils flared to catch the bright scent that pulls me forwards. I will see it soon I'm sure and with the excitement I seem to be flying across the ground, my legs moving quickly, my paws picking their way silently over and around the little things that stick up from the smooth white surface of the snow. It is as if all that exists is my head with its keen eyes, pointed ears and powerful nose and everything else is moving towards it, towards my open mouth where the air rushes over my tongue and through my teeth.

The snow has started to fall again and the day suddenly becomes darker. The wind gusts and I smell more of the beast

– I smell its health and strength and also that it is very close, and so I slow my pace. I look ahead to the mass of trees, watching the spaces in between, and then I see it, a large dark shape moving slowly along, its front end lower as with head down it plods forwards, sniffing the ground for food. I walk beside it, separated by a hundred trees, the beast moving steadily along and not knowing that I move with it and am watching it, trying to judge the power of its legs, the strength of its neck and the size of its spirit. But I am too far away to see these things, so I shorten the distance between us, slowly moving towards it, coming closer like a tree's shadow as the sun rises.

I have crept close enough to see the fur on the beast's neck when it stops walking, its head rising quickly on the end of its thick neck, its large brown eyes and wet nostrils sucking in the space around it. It must know that I am here, though I have made no sound. Sometimes it is like this with them – they stop to listen when you have made no sound, they pause and sniff when the wind carries your scent away, they look yet you are hidden and as still as a stone. But they sense you still, like the deepest root of a tree feeling a sparrow land on the highest branch.

Admirable great beast. And watching her as she searches for

3

me I feel a surge of something in my chest that is like a hunger but not in my stomach. It is a thing that I always feel when I face these creatures. A thing I do not understand but that I know makes me different from other living things, different from the trees and from the snow, more like fire, more like autumn than summer. It begins like this. It ends in many ways but it always begins like this and boldly, feeling as if I am part of the silence of the forest, I step out from behind the tree where I am hidden to face her.

She still searches for a moment, her head and ears revolving slowly around before she spots me. Her head rises a little higher and her eyes lock on to mine. They do not show any fear. Now it is as if all the trees have disappeared, as if there is nothing between us except the length of the other's stride, and no sounds apart from the other's breaths and heartbeats, which we cannot hear, but hearing our own think that we do. We stand motionless and face each other, the snow falling on our backs and everything still and peaceful. But this is an illusion, as seeing the other we both know that the air is charged with scent and danger, that soon where there was silence there might be screaming, and pain where there was stillness.

Her eyes tell me that she is old, but still strong. I see in them a flash of images, her memories, the things she wants me to see. I see where she has come from and where she has been, that she has raised many calves, that she has fought with many wolves and never been brought down to be torn open and eaten. She is telling me that she is not ready for death, that she will still fight and will kill me if she gets the chance. This is what she wants me to see and looking at her still powerful body, her fur that is full and her eyes deep and clear, I know that she doesn't lie and is not ready for death. Sometimes when they are old or very young and frightened they beg for death and only pretend to struggle, and after a short chase it is easy to bring them down and tear them open, not their throats but their bellies.

But this one I know will be different. She is ready to fight, and knowing this I feel that surge in my chest and the hunger in the pit of my stomach. The beast's eyes are beautiful and defiant and in response I tell her that I am young and strong and that though I haven't eaten in many days, although my bones poke a little from under my fur, I am powerful enough to try and take her life from her.

And I wonder at what the beast must feel as she looks into

5

my eyes, because I know where I have come from and what I am, for I am the wolf, the taker of life: the predator. I attack with my eyes open and see death bright and fierce leap in the glance of my prey. I am the wolf, the shadow that brings the light of death, the life that delivers freedom to the fearful, toiling herds and ends the suffering of their weak. I have been with many to hear their last breaths, to hold them, to bring them down, to rip them as they moan and fight for the life which they had discarded and forgotten to live, to warm and reawaken them finally within the fire of its end.

All this I show the beast in an instant, and although she knows that I am alone and have no pack to help me bring her down, she is afraid. Watching her, I too am a little afraid. She is old and past the age where her strength would be impossible to match, but I am weakened by lack of food from this long and desperate winter, so we are well matched and it will be a worthy hunt. We stare at each other for a moment longer and in that moment see all of the other's strengths and weaknesses. The decision is made. She turns and begins to move away through the trees and I follow, unhurriedly, as the chase has only begun.

My eyes on the dark brown shape moving in between the grey trees and over the white snow, and moving steadily so that I am not too close and the beast is never too far away, I am soon lost in that other place where all is quiet but very clear. I have stood on the stillest of these winter days, stopping to listen and thinking that I hear nothing. But the more I have waited the more I have heard – the tiniest of sounds emerging from the silence – a branch creaking or falling to the ground with a distant thump, the call of a bird, the scratching of an insect deep inside a dead tree's wood. I only hear these sounds when I have no need to hear them, as if they know that because I'm not listening for them they can make themselves heard. And now it is the same as I follow the beast. With all my attention on the slowly trotting figure ahead I can hear everything else in the forest around me, a lake of sounds on which rains the patter of her footfalls and my own.

And the forest itself, the mass of sleeping trees and white snow covering everything, the ice hanging down from broken and twisted branches like teeth in a ruined mouth. Does the forest listen to our movement? Do the trees feel in their roots the beast's hooves as she trots along over them? Do they feel the silk of my fur as I slip under one of their branches and shiver in their sleep, knowing what is going on for those who are still awake in the cold, still being hunted and afraid of a death that follows them quietly, eyes like fire and a pink tongue nestled between long sharp teeth? No they cannot know of this, and moving between their trunks I am proud to be awake and alive when they are not, and so must the beast. She must feel more alive now than she has in days.

CHAPTER 2

The day is beginning to get dark when I decide to test her. She has kept a steady pace and shown no weakness in her movement – she has not panicked and tried to bolt away and she hasn't slowed down through tiredness. I have followed patiently behind her but now I quicken, going from a trot to a slow loping run and moving out more to the side than behind her so that she will see me in the corner of her eye, a grey shape slipping through the darker grey of the trees. She sees me and her head turns slightly as she moves. Her eye sees both of mine and in that moment I let her see it, I let her see the flashing teeth and ripped bellies of other beasts like her, the slashed necks of deer, the blood and my hunger for it all and my hunger for her. And it is easy to show her this, because I am hungry in my stomach and the blood in my chest is warm and flowing, pushing me after her, telling me that each kick into the snow is natural, is what I am.

The beast breaks from her trot into a run, the brown shape ahead lurching forwards, the sound of her hooves on the snow suddenly becoming louder and less regular as she quickens. She is wise enough not to panic and run as fast as she can – instead settling into a lumbering canter that although seems slow is fast enough that I have to work a little to keep up. If the beast did bolt now it would be easier. That was my hope when I showed her the kills of my past, the pain that I have delivered of teeth tearing at soft underbelly – because if she were to bolt now her muscles would tire much sooner than mine and I would have the advantage to try and bring her down.

But this beast is old and experienced and thinks that as long as we are both running she has a chance. If I were to try to attack now, if I were to run in and begin snapping at the back of her legs, she might very well still have the power to turn sharply and beat me away. So I let her run on. I don't move in to use my teeth just yet because although she hopes to tire me she does not know that the more she tries to push me away, the more she tries to keep the distance between us, the stronger I will become.

That is the mistake that the stronger ones always make. They believe that the fiercer and more determined they are to fight me off, the more discouraged they will make me. But the more they fight the more I hunger to bring them down. And this one that I follow now through the grey end of this winter's day will soon be far more tired, far weaker than I. This is how I have found it has always been with them, these creatures, and though they can still be dangerous and strong even at their weakest – even at the end of the longest, hardest chase when they may still escape – it is always I that ends with the fullest heart, my lust for death greater than their will to live.

We run like this together for some time, one shape following another through the trees, the day getting gloomier around us as night falls. The forest is filled with the sound of the beast's footfalls, heavy and thumping, the lighter whisking of my paws over the snow and loudest of all her breathing which comes like a heartbeat from ahead, steady and deep. I am beginning to tire. I know that she must be tired too and so I slow my pace, knowing that she will without realising slow down as well – and she does, until we have resumed the brisk trot of earlier. And once we have plodded into the dark of the beginning of night it is as if the effort of earlier had never been. But now we are a little more aware of each other, and I imagine with a sudden excitement that the beast must be a little more frightened than she was before.

Moving as slowly as this I soon feel rested, the tiredness seeping from my legs out into the darkness between the trees, perhaps into the sleeping trees themselves. It is a beautiful night – cold and clear with a sliver of moon to light the way – and knowing that I follow prey I breathe the air in deeply, smelling the wood and snow and above this the beast's scent trailing over the ground in encouragement. I am content to keep my distance until the very depth of the night, when the moon has become hidden and even with my sharp eyes I must focus to pick my way over the ground. And then when it feels as if the night is as dark as it will get I lower my head, my mouth opens and my teeth, poking out beneath my nose, feel the coldness in the air as silently I move forwards from a trot into a run.

This time I don't want her to see me coming. I listen carefully to find out exactly where she is and then I choose my path through the trees, moving rapidly between their trunks, following a path that will hopefully keep me hidden from the corner of her eye. The sound of hooves gets louder as I near but their rhythm stays the same. I am moving very quickly and must be gaining on her with every kick, and a few paces further I see again what I had lost in the darkness, the beast moving steadily ahead – a blurred shape moving in the black of the forest night but appearing in my wide eyes as clear as if it were day. It is difficult to fool these creatures into thinking that you are still only trailing them, especially when you are as close and moving as fast as I am now, yet perhaps she doesn't know how close I am and with excitement I surge forwards into a sprint, dashing between the trees towards her, my paws suddenly pattering loudly on the snow.

These beasts though have strange powers, because she too has already broken into a full gallop by the time I hear the sound of my own paws. I feel the ground tremble and the air is suddenly thick with the noise of powerful hooves crashing down, hurtling the beast forwards, muscle and bone close to breaking as she panics. But even though she is moving quickly, even though I am gladdened by the speed shown ahead of me, I am even more satisfied with how quickly I bear down on her, how easy it is to gouge my legs into the snow and bring her closer with every leap until I am right behind her, the sound of beaten snow deafening, her hooves so close that I must dodge around them as they slam downwards.

Knowing how close I am the beast attempts to turn, but with the trees growing this thickly she does not have the room. She is hesitating, making small changes in direction, searching for a place large enough in which she will be able to stand and fight, and I follow easily, my head cocked to one side as I run, my jaws open and ready and matching her movements so as not to get trampled. She hesitates again and I leap forwards, going for the back of her leg, feeling the muscle flex against my head as I swivel and dig my teeth into it. They hold, fixed in the fur and skin, but only for a moment before I feel them rip away, bringing with them the taste of blood. I keep running but in the moment that I land the beast kicks out with her hoof. I am trying to leap away when the blow lands on my shoulder, pushing me backwards and outwards away from her.

In the instant that I stumble and have to fight to regain my balance I know that the blow she landed was a good one. There is hardly any pain and I have lost none of my will for the hunt, but as I try to run after her again I feel a numbness, an unwillingness spreading from my shoulder down into my claws. She has knocked the wind out of me and I gasp for air, watching angrily as she kicks away another length between us while I struggle after her, still kicking powerfully into the ground to push me forwards but my shoulder and foreleg becoming more and more solid so that I can only run in a strange, slow, jerking movement.

The hunger in my stomach, knowing that it might not feed for another day, begins to coil like a sickness in my belly, while the blood in my chest feels hot enough to burst into my head. I try to keep running but I am limping heavily. I have been beaten back many times and still gone on to bring them down, and thinking that my leg will loosen up as I use it I continue after the beast, even though I find that she is not coming closer, but getting further away until she has disappeared completely into the darkness ahead. I hear a low and angry sound that seems to come from between the trees, but which a few steps later I realise is my own frustrated growling. She is getting away and there is nothing I can do to stop it. There is nothing I can do to stop the sound of her footfalls fading into the night, the scent that was rich and everywhere becoming nothing more than a trail on the ground again.

I could try to follow her like this but now that she has panicked she will run very hard for a long time, and I might not sight her again for a few days, by which time, if I have not eaten, she will surely have become the stronger. No, the chance was here tonight on this night – that was the measure of both of us. She has escaped with a single good kick landed, she took the chance when I failed to grab her properly – and where a moment before every step forwards was as natural as the forest itself and the beast and I were locked together like running water, now we are strangely apart and the hunt is over. That is sometimes the way of it.

I slow to a walk and finally stop limping along and just stand, watching the darkness between the trees in the direction I saw her last. The forest has returned to the very quiet of its night and my breaths make the only sound I can hear, clouding around my head as they shoot from my nostrils and curl upwards from between my teeth. There is a small pain in my shoulder where she struck but it is nothing and I know by the morning it will have gone. I am suddenly very tired. I am still hungry, but it too is nothing because I have been hungry for days and will be hungry again in the morning.

But worse than the tiredness and the hunger is the feeling that I have lost – that I had a chance to take a fine beast and failed – and although this makes me angry it also makes me proud, proud in my heart for what I am and proud for what she did to escape what I do. I can still smell her faintly and imagine that I can still hear the quiet sound of her hooves, but I cannot. I stare for a long time at the black space between the trees and it is only when the feeling in my chest has left completely, leaving me nothing but the hollowness of where it was, that I turn away and look for a place to sleep.

CHAPTER 3

When I awake the next day although the sky is grey and I cannot
see the sun I know instantly that I have slept long into the
morning. I rise and stretch and feel that there is still a stiffness
in my shoulder, but no pain. Yawning, I take a few lazy steps
and begin to sense the day around me: the cold, the quiet of
winter, the brooding lifelessness of the forest that is both worrying
and comforting, as while there may be little food to be found at
least only I seem to be searching for it. The ever-present hunger
of winter sits in my stomach quietly, the maker of the bones that
poke beneath my fur and the spit that sits on my tongue, the
thing that has pushed me to standing when I could have slept
until nightfall. I will need to eat, and soon, if I am not to become
far weaker than I should and so I move off, the stiffness in my
shoulder fading, the trees slipping past me quietly.

This is a bad winter. I have seen four before and only one

of them as a youngster, but this is the worst. The snow and cold have crushed the life out of the forest or sucked it away to satisfy its own desperate hunger. Life exists here still, yes, but locked in the hearts of trees as the tiniest of insects, or deep underground the sleeping roots the deer and hare might dig for, but that no wolf can digest. In the treetops the birds are very much alive and they will sit there and chirp as I pass, knowing I cannot reach them, watching me move, a stream of grey beneath, while I look up to them with amber eyes and wonder at what they feed on, insects perhaps, or maybe each other.

Since the last moon I have roamed the forest, taking paths I had thought forgotten, remembering them again without surprise and with little reward except for the occasional startled mouse or sluggish beetle, made homeless from a falling branch, found stranded in a cold lake of snow to be chewed quickly and hastily, the bitter juices bursting in my mouth to almost make me gag but swallowed eagerly nonetheless. And each time that I have thought that the present is more desperate than anything before, I have found some small morsel, a sorry meal to prevent true and dangerous hunger – the type that sinks the body to the ground instead of pushing me forwards angrily and with teeth bared.

But despite there always being another meal to be had, they have been so small that my bones have become steadily sharper beneath my skin, my legs thinner and my fur duller. I have never been this hungry or this weakened and while there is plenty of strength within me I know from somewhere deep inside that I must eat soon, and well. If I don't I will change – I will change to something less than what I should be, a change that might be impossible to alter.

And moving steadily over the snow and through the trees I am suddenly hit with a wave of regret that I did not make more of the beast last night. If I had got my teeth into her side properly, if I had swerved quicker to avoid the kick, if I had had the will to keep after her no matter how slowly. Could that missed bite be the turning point of this winter, of my life?

Have I already changed so much, been weakened by this winter to the point where I chose not to follow her even though my injury was only slight? Have I changed unalterably already?

I lengthen my gait, hoping to slip away from regret. And moving in an easy trot soon I have. Soon, while I have not forgotten last night, I feel it slip into the past to become a part of what I am, a memory of a hunter to make me better the next time and to make my mind stronger, despite my tired and weakening muscles. When I face a beast again I will hide the failure from my eyes, but I will show my greater wisdom and they will see this and know it and become more afraid of me than if it had never happened. To think of this makes my step lighter and easier over the soft ground, and now I am moving swiftly, looking around me keenly and smelling everything there is to smell, ready to pick up a trail or sight the smallest of movements.

The sky has darkened to a deeper grey when I decide to stop for a rest. It will snow soon. I can feel the way the day is paused, waiting for the event that although occurring all the time is still a little surprising for me, but not perhaps for the trees who must feel it constantly, their branches creaking under ever more weight. Each time that it snows I am reminded that spring is still far off, that this winter has only begun and still has a long path to run, hungering as it passes for the same life that my stomach cries for, taking life and giving it straight to the earth as gaunt frozen bodies buried under the snow.

The flakes begin to fall, tiny specks of white moving downwards, undisturbed by the windless afternoon. I sit and then lie with paws outstretched, pushing my stomach into the ground to ease the pain of hunger, looking at the snowfall and the trees, the white ground and the dark sky above. This area of forest I have little knowledge of, as it is right on the very edge of the land that I have ever roamed, and I look at the space between the trees nearest me, behind which are more distant deep grey trunks that grow so thickly and stretch for such a distance that they become a wall through which nothing but the tiniest sliver of space is visible. And I realise with a sudden jolt of fear why I have come here, why I have come so far that the land appears in front of me for the first time as a barrier.

I rise quickly and shake the snow from my back. I could rest for longer but if there is the chance that I can find a meal along the paths I know then I must not miss it. To think of what is beyond these paths makes my heart quicken and an uneasiness trickle into the back of my neck.

To think that all these days, moving from one hill, through one valley to another, I have not sensed what it really was guiding me here!

I had hoped to come across something like the beast of last night to give me enough food and strength to return to the places I know better. But I failed to take her and now I am here again, pretending to follow these paths in search of a mouse or hare but all the time being pulled towards the edge of my territory, to the edge of what I know. And standing looking at the trees ahead it is as if their sleep has now turned into a hostile silence. They stand together like a herd, flank to flank, facing me and warning me not to approach. The more I stare the more they become alive and dangerous, until they are no longer a herd but a pack, a pack of grey forms like the giant legs of my kind and I look to the sky above them expecting to see their chests and huge heads staring back at me. But there is only a dull sky and falling snow.

The hunger in my stomach still writhes and bites at me and I begin moving again, neither towards the edge or away from it, walking on an old path that I am sure will prove fruitless. The land here moves upwards, the path following the rise of a hill and slowly winding along its side towards its crest. It is the crest that I fear, or rather what exists beyond the crest in the valley below it, and I move towards it slowly, hoping to be distracted by something moving or a sound or smell from deeper among the trees, something that will call me away from this place and from the crest above. But there is nothing. There is no life here except for me, and though a nervousness now grips my neck and legs I continue forwards, the cold emptiness in my stomach pushing me onwards. I place each step as if through water, as if I am swimming in my own craving and have no choice but to reach the other side and clamber out.

The land becomes steeper and my breaths cloud as I climb, the snow deep and becoming loose in clods to tumble quietly behind me. Another few steps and I am at the crest, standing on the spine of the hill, the forest thick behind me but only a few trees growing ahead, the spaces between them large and showing the dark sky behind. To be here so close has turned my nervousness to excitement, the hunger I feel matched by a sudden taste of spit on my tongue. Standing, staring ahead, I think that I could turn away now and return to the inner forest – I could take the chance that I would come across a meal on my way back. Or, I think, swallowing, I can walk a few steps further, to the last of those trees ahead. And even when I get to those trees I can still turn back, back to what I know, to what I am and should be.

I take a few steps forward and with the last of the trees at my side look down into the valley below. Here nothing grows; instead there is just a sheet of snow rolling away from me that cups the last of the day's glow in a weak light, brighter than the stars above that begin to show themselves in the pools of sky between the clouds. Beyond the valley the forest resumes, covering the hills that grow in the distance to become mountains, huge jagged shapes across the land that I watch disappear into the evening sky, fading quickly as if visions. And when the mountains are gone my eyes fall again into the valley and upon a farmhouse, the lair of man that sits large and unmoving like a cluster of stones, smoke trailing upwards from its centre and a soft yellow light seeping from its sides out into the growing darkness. I stand here not with admiration at what man has made, and not with any awe at the strangeness of his home with its straight lines and sharp corners, but with contempt for the shell in which men hide, dead as the stone from which it is made, so different from the merely sleeping trees.

And from here what step do I take? Do I turn and lope off into the forest, into my territory, hoping to find something alive that I might hunt and all the time growing weaker with every step? Or do I go down there, towards that thing in the valley, into a dangerous place where there is no need for hope but only the will necessary to overcome the fear and disgust I feel? My instinct tells me to turn away and run back to the paths I know. But this hunger in my belly, the excitement in my chest and legs screams silently for danger, for the farmhouse below and the thrill of crossing a barrier I shouldn't – a trespass that will surely give me the food that I desire more than anything else. If things were different I would not be here, I would never have come here. But I am here and starving and I won't turn away because I simply cannot. I cannot let myself become weaker and if it means going down into the valley to eat then I must go.

And so I drop down into the valley, slipping smoothly over the hillside as if the shadow of a cloud running quickly beneath a bright moon. My head lowered I feel the coiled strength of my body, of the hunger rising up from my paws to the blades of my shoulders, along my outstretched neck and into the tips of my teeth. The air is cold and thick and I slice through it, the tiniest of pattering on the snow beneath me, the patchwork of cloud and black sky above, the steep hill sleepily flattening out and the farmhouse ahead with its two large blank yellow eyes watching me as I come for it.

In the bottom of the valley the land becomes completely flat and I skip over it towards the farmhouse, hearing the whispering snow beneath me and in my excitement sensing everything with the brightness and clarity of ice. But I am also wary. Over the freshness of winter, I can smell burning, and worse still the smell of man that instantly makes me nervous. I have come across this smell before in the forest, but then it has been thin and often many days old, while here – here it is fresh and lies as heavily on the land as the snow. I have never been amongst so much of it, and though in the forest coming across a man's trail will worry me for a moment, smelling it so strongly as I do now I know that here there is danger, an unknown danger spread about everywhere like the scent itself.

I reach the farmhouse's side and look up to see where smoke pours out high above and thickly into the air, as if some huge injured beast is struggling to push its last breaths into the night while I, small and quick, slink up to it unnoticed. Silently I move along the wall, the stone rising like a cliff at my side and on the other the white lake of snow stretching back up towards the forest. I think I hear something and freeze, my paw in mid-air, but all I sense is the sound of my own nervous heart clicking in my chest and the whisper of breaths that cloud around my head and in the air before me. I step lightly, edging nearer to the large yellow eyes high in the stone. And as I pass under these eyes I stop and look up into them and imagine I see fear in that pale yellow glow – the frightened stare of the exhausted beast, watching helplessly as the wolf comes to bite at her soft stomach.

I look away and continue along the wall to its end. I lengthen my neck and stretch it slowly around the corner to see the place where the sheep are kept, a small area attached to the farm-house, a short distance away from where I stand half-hidden. I wonder if any of them are awake, if even now one of them can see an alien shape of pointed ears and shining eyes, as if the edge of stone itself has grown a head to look at them. But none of them stirs and I step around the corner, suddenly moving into their rich scent that both excites me and disgusts me. Behind the tangle of sticks that keeps them captive they appear as milky shapes in the dark, huddled and sleeping among themselves, the cold and the heavily falling snow. And through the snow I move towards them, a dark shape in the night, hunger burning in my stomach.

As I get closer their shapes become more distinct. Instantly I distinguish the large from the small and the thin from the weak, which ones probably limp when walking. But tonight there will be no careful selection. Against these creatures I cannot measure myself as a hunter, because they are man's crea-tures, beasts he has tortured to give up their wildness and made ugly by stripping them of their instinct, other than huddling foolishly together and running in panicked circles. I would rather eat the carrion of something wild than take one of these

29

sheep, and if I had the strength tonight I would kill them all, not in frenzy but because I hate their weakness, as all wolves do, our loathing and fear of man and what he has done found at dawn in a hundred bloodstained bodies, appearing wilder in death than they had been in life.

These thoughts pass as quickly as an angry breath and suddenly I am at the fence, gazing at a round bulge of flesh that is leaking through the sticks towards me. I cannot tell what part of the sheep it is but that doesn't matter – not here against these creatures – just as long as I can get my teeth into it. So I sink my body down into my paws, the ground feeling as firm and readied as the teeth hidden beneath my curling lips. I strike forwards and grab the sheep, my snout burying into its hide, and though it takes only an instant I feel a brief resistance before the power of my jaws punctures the sheep's thick skin and sends my teeth piercing into the flesh beneath.

The silence is shattered as the sheep screams in pain and fear. It lurches violently to its feet and I see its head rise above its body and turn to face me, its mouth open in a constant cry, its eyes swollen with sudden terror. As it twists and tries to pull itself from my jaws I pull back with all my strength, spreading

my paws on the ground and wrenching backwards, not caring whether I pull the whole thing through the fence or only tear off a mouthful. The other sheep are panicked and all of them bleating loudly, but I don't care for them or the sudden end of my stealth because I can feel the sheep coming towards me – I am pulling it or a part of it through the fence, all teeth barbed terribly in its flesh. And with each wrench I can feel something tearing, perhaps the wood of the fence, or perhaps the creature's leg from its back – a wonderful ripping that is smoother and longer with every tug.

Suddenly there is a bright yellow light. It floods everything before touching me and leaping into my eyes – a blindness, but only for an instant before shapes begin to reappear around me hazed and golden. I pull on the sheep, but weakly now because I am confused by the light and a little afraid, as there should be no light, unless between standing on the hillside and coming down into this place I have somehow gone through the night. And now there is another sound, murmuring at my side beneath the screams of the sheep. I tilt my head to look in its direction and there in the light through the brush of the sheep's fleece is a huge shape coming towards me, the sounds becoming more distinct and out of the brightness suddenly attaching themselves to its movement.

Footfalls, coming towards me! And with them the horrible smell of man. I open my jaws and shake the beast from them, swerving away from the fence and the thing approaching me. My front paw slips in the snow and I fall forwards, my head crashing into the ground and snapping my open mouth shut with a clack. I can hear the man coming very close now and try to stand, twisting my body in the snow until all the ground is beneath me and I can push upwards to face him, standing before him with head lowered, seeing the shining in his eyes and the long black stick of his gun.

He is coming for me and raising his gun and though I know I am surely dead and would like nothing more than to fly through the air towards his throat, something more powerful makes me turn and start running, running so fast that I think I will trip and fall, my legs a mess of movement. And then the crack in the air that pounds against all the other noises and I wait for pain or death but it doesn't come and I keep running. A second crack in the air and now I am going upwards towards the forest and the noise is less shattering. The hill becomes steep but I keep running, a force I have never known pushing me upwards until the openness has ended and I am in among the trees.

I stop and turn, safe with the trees around me and their thick trunks and branches clasped protectively above. The snow has stopped falling and I can see back down into the valley where the man staggers among his sheep, going from one to the other with outstretched arms of false tenderness, whispering comforting sounds to calm them – the same sounds he will utter when they feel the slicing blade against their throats. The sheep are still panicked and running from him as they would me, but they calm as quickly as the snowfall has ebbed and he is able to handle each in turn, searching for marks of my attack.

I watch this unpleasant scene while I wait for my heart to calm, for my breaths to lessen. I have never run so fast! What power I still have in me that I could run up that hill so quickly! I think that I will turn and walk into the forest, but hesitate. I want to be sure of what I am seeing down there. I want to be sure that it is good that I am still here alive on this hillside, and so I stare again at the farmhouse and the tiny shapes moving about, willing a feeling of well-being to form in me. But none comes because I know that something happened that is very wrong, and as I am about to turn away again I realise what it is — it is that I was afraid, that the force I felt was not my own power but something placed in me by man. Even as I stand here hesitating, alive and able to live for another chance at killing, I do so for the first time as the hunted, as the thing feeling its own life instead of ripping it from another.

Terror! That was the force that made me streak up the hillside like lightning, back into the safety of these trees.

And even as I turn and begin to move back into the forest I feel it behind me, that awful feeling of fear, the horror of something inescapable. Perhaps this is how the beast feels when I walk behind her in the river she sadly ploughs through the snow, knowing that the enemy will not give up, knowing that to stop once to rest will mean to never start again. I walk quickly on and know that nothing is following me but my own feelings — there is no man hunting me, there is no death that will fall tonight like a broken branch to thump against the snow. But the terror that I felt — to me that is more real than any gun or hunger, and I walk long towards dawn until I know I can walk no more and must find a place to sleep, the sky becoming grey and the birds beginning to sing, an awful sound.

CHAPTER 4

I wake to find that the snow has stopped and the day is bright. Snow has covered me in the night and I rise and quickly shake it off, stretching and yawning with stiff limbs, blinking with sleep-filled eyes to see the day around me – a perfect winter's day, no wind, the air bright and clear and smelling fresh and clean and everything radiant from the bright yellow sunlight drenching it all, gleaming on the white-blue snow and sparkling in the ice that hangs from the trees. I stand among the bright and silent stillness, hearing nothing, smelling only the clean air of the forest and feeling the first shards of warmth find their way through the fur on my snout – a warmth so delicate that any movement and it would be lost – and as I stand with pleasure in the sunlight I know that I can last another day.

Usually on a day like this I would laze around and stretch and roll in the snow. I would stand or lie still, so as to let every part of my body be warmed by the sun, I would close my eyes and let its brightness dazzle me, I would listen intently for the quiet sounds within the stillness and think of nothing except for what my senses gently perceived. But already I can feel the coil of hunger in my stomach. And with it comes a sudden flush of fear and shame and I remember what happened last night, how I had been afraid – chased up that hill with an empty stomach.

Now the two are joined together – my hunger and my fear, and I know I must eat to stop the other from seeping deep into me and rooting, to take hold and drag me down like a vine a tree. Whatever occurred last night it cannot be undone. It was a shock to feel such things but I am still alive and while I have this life no matter how weak I become I will continue forwards. As nothing can outrun me, no fear or memory will be able to keep pace, to follow the paths I take from here.

Perhaps, too, I will come across that man's fresh scent in the forest, deep in the forest, near the night, him lost and blinded and seeing shapes everywhere darting between the trees. I hope for this. And so I move off, slowly at first, feeling my body loosen as I go, a heat growing from inside me and spreading right to the tip of my tail, warmer than the distant sun.

Really there is no reason to be afraid. In the forest, among the trees, moving quickly as I do now a wolf fears no man. I have seen men trample and hack their way through, grunting with effort, sometimes falling over, noisily fighting against the resistance of dense bushes and plants or staggering in the deep snow. They are blind to the paths I take — they cannot skip over the ground in the never-ending movement of a wolf's gait, shadowlike in its solitude, movement often for its own joy and without meaning or purpose. These trees of my home men see as barriers, the snow they see as a hindrance, the bitter cold and biting wind an enemy — but I love these things because they are what makes me strong, they do not pull me down but have always pushed me on, as they do now, away from the memory of man.

I move deeper into the forest, becoming more alert to what is around me, quickly distancing myself from the previous night. But each time I think of what happened a flicker of fear rushes around my chest and stops my breath. As I trot along I force myself to think of it, of the way the man had stood before me and how I thought I would be killed, and of the panicked run up the hillside. I force myself to remember as if grinding down the end of a bone, each time resistance, each time something there but with every repetition a lessening, until it is almost completely gone. Maybe the fear I felt merely came from the shock, from it being unknown and novel.

But did he spare me? Could he have killed me and chosen not too? He was stood right in front of me and lowering his gun – when I slipped he had every chance and yet I am still here, passing over this land that is now just a blur as I look inwards, as I try and digest the emptiness that I feel on thinking that he could have killed me but didn't. I should have gone for his throat! I should have ripped him apart there and then for his hesitation. But I couldn't. Perhaps he knew the fear he had put in me and knew that I could only run. Maybe that is why he didn't kill me, not to spare my life, but to mock me. Well, now I have learned and will not be afraid the next time, when it is not so new.

The trees sprouting grey and slender from the white ground seem to be moving past me rather than I them. Then, following the path that bends around one of their number it is as if the snow suddenly leaps up in front of me, startling me so that my next step is more a leap into the air instead of one forwards and I am dragged back into the world from my thoughts. And this living snow turns in the air revealing long legs and long ears and then the flash of an eye very frightened.

A hare! I think, as the shape twists before me slowly, its pure white body held by the thickness of the cold air, its legs tangled but untangling themselves as it falls to land on the ground. With mouth open I lunge forward to catch it, but startled and having hesitated the hare has already landed and leaped to the side by the time I am close and my teeth crack together holding nothing. Now the hare bursts forwards in a bounding run and I am after it, all thoughts lifting as my paws hit the crunching snow beneath, my hunger and tiredness vanishing, suddenly replaced with the complete joy of my intent.

Ahead the hare runs in a low and balanced scamper and I follow closely, seeing nothing but its white shape as it weaves across the sheet of covered ground, leaning gracefully as it turns, leaping magnificently upwards and to the side to escape my flashing jaws that clack shut sharply above the sound of trampled snow. I follow and am led, led by the vibrant life before me, the life that I have given. We run and jump together in the yellow sunlight over the snow for only an instant – or half a day, neither of us will know until it has ended but now we are inside it, inside something that is whole and contains the forest and the ground deep beneath. The hare may escape and has a good chance because weakened I am tiring, and if it does escape it will sleep deeply tonight knowing today it has lived, knowing today that a wolf followed its beautiful movement, its arcing jumps and quick sharp turns and it, the hare, ran from me and was not taken.

But on one of its sharply twisting turns the hare stumbles, a small white foot slipping outwards without grip, its whole body jolting downwards from the mistake. As the white shape tumbles and overturns in the snow I feel a flash of sorrow for its fall: the glancing sadness for the instant of every chase's end, be it the crashing slump of the torn and hamstrung beast, or as now a wrong step after many quick and sure. But this moment is short and has ended by the time I am in the air, leaping now knowing that the hare cannot dart away, watching it flail and spin helplessly against the air and the snow.

I land front paws first that clamp the hare and shove it roughly into the ground, and as I bring in my jaws I see the small black eye looking at me with terror and understanding, all the spirit of its darting run replaced by weak and hated consent, meekness clouding where before must have been defiance, and unhesitatingly my jaws flash forwards – I feel the crunching of small bones – then the hare is lying slumped and unmoving.

I eat calmly – I have no brothers with which to compete and nothing else would dare try take my meal. I do not even worry for the annoyance of the black crows that would usually observe my feeding from the branches above, calling loudly to each other. The forest is so empty that even they are absent today and besides, with a small kill like this they would be left with nothing. With just a few bites the terrible gnawing hunger of many days is gone, and the remainder I chew slowly, not wanting to speed towards the point where there will be one bite left, and then nothing. The hare's largest bones are easy to crack and soon nothing is left but a red smear on the white ground, a smear still charged with scent that I sniff hazily as if there were more meat to be had.

The sun is still shining from an almost cloudless sky and imagining its warmth I stretch and roll in the snow, relieved that at last I have rid myself of hunger, grateful that for the moment at least I don't need to push wearily on in search of food. Rising, I shake off the snow that has clung to my fur, and after lazy wanderings find a place in which to rest. Turning in a circle once I sink to the ground and curl my tail over my head, seeing the brightness of the sun through closed eyes, hearing nothing from the trees around me and feeling the first rays of wonderful warmth reach through my coat to my skin as I lie without thinking and feel myself gently lost in sleep.

CHAPTER 5

The sun has moved in the sky and I find myself in shadow when sleep ends and I am pushed back up into the world. Chilled, I stretch and stand and feel a fresh wind stir over the ground to take away the stillness of the afternoon. In the sky the clouds are gathering and little blue is left, the yellow light of the afternoon replaced almost everywhere by more familiar grey, and where the sunlight does remain it moves between the shifting clouds in patches that fade and disappear, only to reappear and fade somewhere else.

The temperature is dropping and already I am hungry. It is as if the hare, the sunlight, the warmth and satisfaction of earlier never existed. Their memory is worthless when compared to what I feel now – hungry again, afraid for my thinning muscles, tired but with no choice but to move on.

It is like this after a small kill. In winter I live with hunger almost constantly – this winter more than ever – and I become used to it until I eat and it goes away and only then, when it is not there, do I worry that it will return. But it has always been the same. A hare is too little and soon I am hungry, while with a beast I eat too much and bloat myself until I feel I'll never want to eat again.

What I would give to gorge on a beast in the heat of midsummer! Now, cold and hungry, I long for its richness. Yet on hot summer days, when the heat is inescapable even in the shade of the tallest trees, I long for the distant coolness of winter. It is my nature – unlike the deer or sheep who meekly graze their mouthfuls of delicate grass – to wander between too much and not enough.

I begin again through the trees, listening to my muscles, searching in the movement of my body for the extra strength given by the hare's life. It was a small meal, a few mouthfuls, perhaps only slightly more than if I had eaten my own tail, but it is there inside me – that bounding run, those jumps and quick movements and finally the sweet-tasting blood and bone. Maybe my eyes are sharper now, my step quicker and lighter so that the next I come across will have less chance than before.

And this also I love – the grey of a normal winter's day, the darkening gloom of a covered sky, the snow threatening to fall as I pad on the dull white ground, climbing with it as it slopes upwards, rising onwards and higher until the woods and valleys appear in view around me, sunken and distant, greyed by the end of day. The ground flattens slightly and I lope forwards, and soon I am at the peak of a hill, the land all around me stretching dimly into the distant horizon, the hills and valleys a rolling sea of pale lifelessness. Far off the clouds are still broken, the sun bursting through with thick bars of light that form pools of brilliance among the gloom, but still do nothing to give life to the land crushed so brutally by this winter.

In spring and summer all this is green and blue and dotted with the bright colours of flowers, and everywhere is alive and moving and unafraid to be seen. But now everything is hiding, as if the land itself has put its head behind its wing like a bird, stopping the winter from looking in, making sure it cannot itself look out. I look over the myriad trees beneath me, white-specked grey trunks spiking from the white earth, wondering at the dull life locked so deeply away inside them, hoping to see a flicker of something else through their branches that might betray movement of some kind.

I remain standing and looking into the forest for a long time. When I look up to the horizon I see that the pools of sunlight have moved away to become tiny yellow dots in the distance. I have seen nothing stir and drop my head, tiredness aching in my neck and the emptiness below me seeming to echo in my head – the sound of another fruitless ploy to find food. Quickly I feel the impulse to move on, to be in a different place from here where there might be life. I look to where I know the path lies between the trees below and lift a paw to step towards it off the hillcrest, and it is just as I begin to move forwards that I see a branch fall from a tree to drop silently onto the ground.

I pause, fascinated by the movement. After staring at blank stillness for so long I am entranced, amazed that something happened, even if it was only another broken bough, one of many and nothing important. But for a moment I cannot look away. My desire to find anything other than nothing is so strong that I am gripped, paw still hanging at an angle from my leg, moving as slowly back to the ground as my dreamlike thoughts laze around what was seen. And then, still in my dream, I watch

47

as the branch floats back up into the air, hangs there for a moment, and then attaches itself to another tree.

Mouth closing I bring my head up in a smooth fast movement, my ears shooting forwards and locked like my eyes on this new strange branch. And when it fell, it fell silently, did it not? It is not so far away that I couldn't have heard it and so now I am suspicious, alert, eager, my heart beating strongly in my chest. All my attention is on the branch, or where I thought I saw it appear. So fixed is my gaze that it is as if everything I see is loose and slippery before me. Then something is dropping to the ground again, but instead of falling swoops upwards at the last moment to attach itself to another tree – I see wings spreading to balance the landing, the thin branch swaying up and down with the novel weight of this black, feathered snowfall.

A crow. Annoying scavengers; unintelligible mockery from the treetops as they sit there watching for what scraps I might leave. And it is like fish in a stream – once you spot one, the rest appear as if suddenly uncovered and now I can see many of them, small black shiny objects among the branches, moving silently from one tree to another, moving as a group, as a pack, moving towards something. I dig my back legs in and launch myself down the hillside, sliding in the steep bank of snow that is forgiving and lets me plummet down towards the forest, towards where the birds are moving to.

I reach flatter ground and collect my balance, bringing my paws under me and stretching out my gait into a large easy lope. I am not following a beast or a hare but a prospect, the prospect that the crows moving as one are following something, and while it is only a chance and not enough to bring spit to my mouth it is enough of a chance that my tiredness is lost in excitement. Perhaps they are following a hare, or even a deer! How a deer now would strengthen me – I would not need to eat again for days!

And as I move towards nothing for certain I imagine the perfection of the deer that might stagger feebly ahead: the wonderful tastes, the textures of the rich meat, the smells left on the bloody snow and the beautiful lake-like depth of two brown eyes and their last flicker of life. It becomes as powerful in my thoughts as sensation and I run faster, feeling that what I dream for is true and so clear that it must exist ahead among the trees.

When I hear one of the crows call nearby I slow to a silent

trot. I cannot already have come far enough to be among them but must be on the edge of their number, and so my gaze shifts to the branches overhead, searching for their shiny forms. Low slanting bars of yellow sunlight catch my breath and hold it in golden clouds that I pass through and leave behind, the bright light glaring straight at me and making it difficult to see. But then I spot one of the birds, not in the treetops but sitting quietly on a lower branch, facing away from my approach, then quickly departing with a rustle towards the call of another ahead.

I follow with a quick trot that quietens to a walk again when I see another bird. And not only one, but another after it further on, and perhaps even another, although from this distance I might be mistaken. But these three shapes are forming a line, a rough and bending line in front of me towards what must be the event,

and I move forwards, starting quietly but quickly thundering towards the first bird that sees me and shrieks from the treetop. It shrieks again from behind me as I pass it, and as I approach the second I can see a third and a fourth, a line unravelling before me faster than I can chase it down, leading me down into a dip and then up a small hillside, horrible sounds of fluttering wings, screams and the fury of small creatures rising from the other side.

I reach the top of the mound and see below me a mass of black wings and beaks flashing down at something on the ground, swooping down in turn to peck and stab at their prey before retreating upwards again to the branches above. Some of the crows have seen me paused at the mound and are screaming with fear, but their cries go unnoticed by the others – the others who are too filled with the hunt to care for anything else. I hesitate because I wonder what it is they are attacking. It is too large for a hare – besides the patches of coat I see between the black wings are red or brown and not white – but it is too small for a deer, even a small deer and the season for their young passed long ago. Each time it struggles to regain its footing and take a few staggering steps, the crows plunge and beat it to the ground, falling on it in endless shrieking waves that force it tumbling onto the snow.

But more of the birds have noticed me now approaching cautiously down the mound towards the mob, and with fewer birds attacking their prey is becoming uncovered, its body becoming visible behind their dark forms like a red sky emerging from rain clouds, a snarling head appearing with pointed ears that are ragged and bleeding, then a tail tipped with white, and a small body much like my own, but punctured and bloodied with wounds from the crows' beaks.

Not a deer but a fox! – I realise with shock. What perversion is this, that crows could be hunting a fox, a predator like me? If I were to become weaker, would they dare to hunt me as well? Only from this winter could things such as this be made real! My own failed begging of sheep from man; crows coming together to kill a fox. It is this crippling winter and its constant shadow of hunger that forced me against my nature – these birds must be starving as well to hunt the fox and go against theirs.

And here I was expecting a meal and instead I am given a fox, a mere competitor that must be killed and will bring little satisfaction to my stomach. I hesitate for a moment, caught in disappointment and the change of situation. Then I rush forwards from the mound, each gouge into the ground stoking my anger, all this effort now so pointless and forced on me rather than desired. I must kill the fox to prevent him from ever catching something I might myself pursue, and even as I run towards the mess of wing and feather pounding at the small predator I feel a rage boil within me that the fox is here in my territory, and worse, that its presence caused me to dream, to fantasise about something that didn't exist – a horrible exposure of how weak and foolish I have become.

The crows must hear me coming as they all begin to rise up away from the fox in a screaming black cloud. But I am moving so quickly that I flash through the air and can bring my jaws snapping shut on the flapping bodies that are too slow to escape, feeling their brittle bones snap like thin ice as first I crush one

bird and then another. As I land my chest crashes into the side of the fox and sends it flying backwards, rolling and tumbling over in the snow. It comes to rest and turns its head, its eyes wide with terrified surprise while it raises a single paw in futile hope to fend me off. I leap again and come down upon its body that twists sideways on the ground, half to shield itself and half in submission – I smother it with my paws and lunging forwards catch its throat between my teeth.

In my grip the fox lies limp, surrendering totally, offering no resistance or fight. I squeeze with my jaws and feel the taut flesh of his neck tense instinctively, but still he neither writhes nor flails and instead lies still in submission, knowing that any struggle would cause me to keep on squeezing and choke him. I hold him, hearing his breaths whistle from between his clenched teeth and foaming nostrils, then quickly I release my grip and swing my head with bared teeth to above his own, which looks up at me with a single terrified green eye.

That eye screams for mercy. Like them all, like they all have done, those that I have stood above and breathed upon, admiring their suffering. But with him his thoughts are stronger, his meaning clearer, for he is a predator like me and although vicious enemies we share something, perhaps even if it is only something against each other, or against man, whose eyes reveal nothing but a jumble – which once I saw unexpectedly from a distance as they stared back at me through the trees, an incomprehensible jumble of thoughts that deafened and confused, while the man, standing without moving, awed by my presence, had recognised in me only the difference between us.

And this fox, there is more than pleading in his eye. He is showing me something, he is giving me something he does not want to but must when faced with the death that stands over him, and again I hesitate, the forest seeming to shift and swim around me, the fox begging for his life and sucking me in with the power of his desperation. And I should be surprised when the green of his eye seems to become that of spring itself and his thoughts the warmer wind after winter, heavy with prospect. But they are predictable in their deceit, these creatures, and I choose not to kill him just yet so that I can enjoy his last, beautiful lies. And perhaps I will soften in my stare and on the hold I have on him so that he thinks he is succeeding. But when I see the hope flash across that bright glistening stone in his head, then I will kill him.

CHAPTER 6

I can feel the fox's ribs beneath my paw, a tiny cage holding his life inside that I could probably crush if I kept on pushing. When he breathes in I push downwards to make him gasp for air, to make him know that his life is over and might be squeezed slowly from him this way instead of the flash of my jaws to tear open his throat. But still he holds my gaze, his green eye sparkling up at me, his thoughts unfurling behind it so quickly that I feel myself becoming confused, dazed with their speed and richness.

He shows me a thin, staggering deer slumping to the ground, no life in its eyes. He shows me the rotting, frozen corpse of a beast and another of his kind greedily devouring its insides. He shows me the land from where he comes – a great plain of snow and rock, lifeless, barren, starved even of trees – and together we move through it, him leading me through his eyes and into his memories and then suddenly we are in the middle of summer, we are together by a lake with the green stalks of every plant brushing at our chins and stomachs – the trees are towering above us more laden with the life of their leaves than they ever are with snow and we look across at the perfect flat gold of water, and in the middle of it a white bird, a huge bird with poised neck and wing and moving across the surface like the surface itself. And seeing this I am filled with blood in my chest, each beat of my heart seeming only to give me more life to remain in the brilliance of the fox's lies.

Yes, beautiful indeed, I think, and press harder on his chest. And now he is really struggling for each breath and I think that I will end it this way, that at any moment I will feel a snap beneath my paw and watch him writhe as the bone splinters and his life is squashed into the snow. But even now his eye is calm as it pleads, his thoughts no longer flying from one place to another and instead showing me a cloud – or is it snow? Snow in the shape of something alive, and feigning interest I lift my paw a little from his chest. The fox sucks in air hungrily and his thoughts suddenly become clearer – he shows me the bird again, the one on summer's lake, but now dead and impossibly large in death, a white mass slumped on whiter ground like an offering.

For an instant I look away from the fox's eye. I can feel a trickling of excitement in my shoulders. When I look back to the fox he has seen that I understand, that I know that he is offering me a meal, this white bird in return for his own life. Clever little cousin, little enemy! You offer what I need most, you show me this bird, this swan – no ordinary bird but one that is large and powerful: and where there is power there is muscle, flesh that could fill my stomach for many days! He is looking up at me still as I think these things and I see a trace of betrayal flicker across his eye, a betrayal not for me but for something else, something hidden or unknown.

He must have buried the bird! The more I stare into his thoughts the less he is able to hide them and with growing relish I begin to see him digging down into the snow, digging a deep hole large enough that he and another would easily be hidden. He had hoped to lure me away from here with the offer of the swan alone, but I have prised from his mind that it is buried, and the betrayal I see is not for me but for his own survival!

Yes, he must be very near to starvation. Despite me pressing

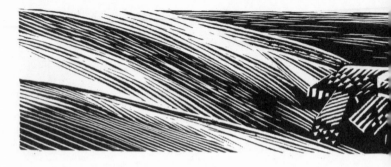

down on him he still believed he could get away and return to this feast, wherever it is, to uncover it and save himself. Brave fox, I admire you! – but even more your demise, because you will lead me to it and I will eat and you will starve. He will die from my intent, but not necessarily my jaws – but I do not show him this – I show him how he will lead and I will follow, and how if he tries to run I will bring him down and tear him open. I show him this and then lift my paw from his side.

He looks at me nervously and rolls slowly upright, then shifting his paws, shaking, begins to stand. He looks away and I watch as he staggers upwards, pushing with his legs to force his gaunt body away from the snow that is freckled with his blood. Then he is standing before me, small and pitiful, looking miserably into the space before him – a space where he will

not see me – and all the while he shakes and trembles in spasms that run from his head through to his thin legs.

He turns his head towards me, but slowly, as if the cold air between us is solid and unyielding. But eventually his eyes meet my own and in them I can see nothing but defeat – there is so much loss and wretchedness in his gaze that for an instant I think I will kill him and step forward quickly with teeth bared, wanting only to take the life away from those eyes. But the coil of hunger in my stomach, the promise of the buried meal, stops me and all that happens is that I watch as the fox falls back to the ground, tripping on his own paws as he tries to skip sideways. I stand over him, my teeth nearly touching his eye, the jets of my furious breath making him flinch. But calmer, I step backwards away from him. He rolls upright again and looks up to me and in that instant the pact is made between us – that he will take me to the bird, that he will lead me to where this swan is buried and has no other choice but death until then.

With this understood between us he clambers to his feet. He is weak – much weaker than me – so I let him eat one of the crows that is broken on the ground behind me, while I eat the other, its body spindly and fleshless, a meal that I would otherwise chew with distaste but now so hungry gulp down gratefully. It is strange to be eating with another, so much like my kind, after so long eating alone and mostly not eating at all. And then with a simple glance I order him to lead, and glancing back he assents completely with dulled eyes, turning once before moving off with cautious steps.

I follow the fox's stumbling gait that quickly smoothes into an effortless march, the easy march like mine behind it which covers any distance, and no man could hope to follow. The afternoon has darkened and the sky is deepening in grey, and snow falls on our backs as with quiet footfalls we move together through the trees. Still the afternoon darkens, and the glowing snow-covered ground seems brighter than the blackening sky, and in the half-light the fox and I, moving one behind the other, sense together the silent moment before the forest becomes another winter's night, the space when all is still, when all seems bound together, indivisible. But enemies, competitors, one the slave of the other, neither of us cares for a sharing glance or signal and we continue our movement, together for a moment, but a few steps later divided.

The fox begins to lead me along pathways I do not know, some of them awkward and not as easy for my larger frame to travel – branches so low that I must scrape my belly to get under them and alleys thin enough that the limbs of bushes and fallen trees claw at my sides. I wonder if he does this on purpose, hoping to get me so tangled or caught in something that he will be able to run. But he does not look back once, and in his gait, within the lightness of step that carries him quickly forward, there still hangs heavily his defeat, and I find that I don't fear him bolting just yet.

By the time it is truly night I am unsure as to what part of the forest we are in. Yet as we travel onwards I begin to recognise my surroundings again. We are off the paths and tracks I know but unmistakable signs in the trees and in the scents give me a vague knowledge of where we are, that we have come in a long looping arc that is now curving dangerously towards where I was last night, where the sheep are – the foul-smelling sheep even a bite of whom I failed to come away with. Annoying, that the fox's route should come close to the open sore of such recent memories.

Still – it is a large valley and makes up a large part of the edge of the land I know, so it is not surprising that we will at some point be near to it. And then I think that perhaps the fox knows of last night. I glance at the fox suspiciously and wonder if he acts with intent, whether he knows of the shameful fear I felt and which I now feel rising in me again. Perhaps he saw it in my eyes when I had him on the ground, or at a moment of rage when I could not hide it, and now he leads me here in an effort to frighten me and use it to his advantage.

But he cannot know! It was I who took from him – I revealed nothing. I am uneasy because we are near to the place, that is all. Should I be uneasy – should I be feeling this horrible nervousness, building with each footfall along this thin and winding path? Would my kind mock me and be disgusted if they knew what I felt, or would they feel the same? Perhaps they would have already spurned me if I had returned to them last night as I was, the faint smell of man beneath my paws and the brighter glint of fear in my eyes. But they are not around and do not know yet and if I feed well and become strong again, surely I will forget it myself.

So I must follow this fox.

We are still quite far from the valley, and I should have no reason to be afraid, but men roam widely in their territories and I find myself hoping not to smell his trail, which now I am beginning to dread – and this shames me. I escaped him, did I not? Yes – yet I was afraid, and no matter that I did survive when the man could have killed me the fear that I felt, new and out of my control, has stayed with me and now it flares in my chest while I fight to rule it, to push it away. And as if in response to my silent struggle behind him the fox leads me out from the path we walk along, away from the frozen branches that have clasped at my flanks and onto the hard-packed snow of a wider trail. He turns onto it and looking back once continues onward, and suddenly I am certain that our bending route will end in an unswerving line towards man's lair, because I know that this path we follow now leads nowhere else.

The land begins to rise upwards in a small hill, a different hill from the night before but leading towards the same valley. Everything is the same, everything is how it should be – the dark mass of trees all around, the cold firmness of the ground, the pure air of winter on which the smells and sounds of the forest slip like ice. The night before I felt these things also, I felt them dripping into my body and my thoughts, strengthening me, altering me only as far as I would let them. But now I cling to them. With horror I find myself hanging on to them as the present – the shape of a tree's bough, the smell of an exposed leaf, the sound of my paw on the hard snow, these things are part of this path, of this time before I am dragged towards what I fear ahead. I must hold them against this nervousness rattling in my chest and legs, that would chatter my teeth if I did not make them bite upon themselves.

I could stop the fox and demand that we take another route. But if I were to do that, if I were to have to face his eyes now, he would surely know where his freedom lay, he would see into my fears and I might not be able to hide that if he were to run headlong into the valley towards the farmhouse – if he were to do it boldly and with head raised, if he were to make it clear to me that he did it knowing that I was afraid – I would never be able to follow him. He could surely escape if he saw those things! So I cannot stop him and must instead cling to these things around me, these things that can only remind me that we are not at the valley yet.

Even though I try to control the icy rivers flowing within me my body is tense and awkward as I follow the smaller hunter, and I am grateful he doesn't look behind him. We continue upwards, and above him, over the curve of his head, between the points of his ears, I can see the open blackness of where the trees end, where the valley must begin, and though fear and nervousness are biting at me sickeningly I keep stepping forwards, almost unsure as to whether my steps are of my own will.

And then the fox has stopped up ahead. He does not look back but below and before him, and I come to stand beside him at the peak of the hill, the forest above and behind us, while below where we both look the valley lies as a rolling sheet of pallid grey in the darkness, open and bare, the farmhouse sitting quietly in its centre like a cluster of rocks.

CHAPTER 7

From the corner of my eye I see that the fox has turned to look at me. Now I must be careful – even though I am afraid I must show no sign, give no signal to release him from his pact and into freedom. And the fear itself I can feel like something alive inside me, pushing, struggling upwards against my will to hold it down. Its edges are loose and soft like biting water, but its force is so strong that if I do not control it I feel sure it will flow from me into the fox's awareness as plainly as a river. I pause, letting my gaze rest on the farmhouse, pretending to assess the sharpness of its form before I turn my head, and even then my eyes remain locked on the high stone walls and wooden fences until with a sudden movement I flick them sideways to meet the fox's own.

I had expected to see in them defiance, barely hidden satisfaction in him having led me to a place where I would be afraid.

But instead I see that he too is afraid – not only is he afraid he is terrified – he is not trying to hide it but seemingly trying to show me as forcefully as possible how much we should be afraid of man. I look at the fox, small and agitated before me, clearly afraid, more afraid of man and the farmhouse below than he is even of me and it is as if all my anxiety has flown from my shoulders onto his to grip and shake him like an eagle a fish.

And seeing this I feel my own fear vanishing, a sudden, wonderful awakening to things other than near terror, the forest and the night rushing back in to fill my senses: senses which before had been clogged with mud as I clung to the present, now filling again with bright scents and excitement. I am lifted with relief! The more I look at him the less fear I feel, and I look at him a long time until I think it must have gone completely – a weakness of the past, another strange but fleeting part of this winter.

The fox stares off towards the other side of the valley for a moment before his eyes return to mine. He wants to get there, to the forest on the other side. We could cut straight across, but instead he is showing me a thin winding path that trails a far way along the edge of the trees. In his fear he is letting me see the route, this long way around to the other side, so clearly that I could almost find it without him. Then he looks down at the farmhouse again but the sight of it makes him so afraid that he cannot look at it for long.

And seeing his terror I wonder how I could ever have been afraid of man. My eyes tell him calmly that we will not go the long way round, and calmly I watch his distress grow, each tremor of his head, each flick of his eyes adding to my daring, feeding the boldness that a few steps behind us I had actually believed might be lost. Man – man and his stinking lair and filthy sheep! I escaped him, did I not? He was close enough to strike yet did not – what is there to fear of man?

The fox now is begging me to go around, but he has no memories to show for his fear, no escape, no fight, no contact with the thing he is so afraid of, and can only keep pleading with me to take the paths of his preference. Again and again he tries to suck me into his thoughts, to show me the few times he has safely taken this route back to his territory. But I merely watch, enjoying his fear. I am tired and hungry, but most of all I am excited. I feel the ground beneath my feet not as something dead and hard but as a force that is pushing me upwards,

that is crying for my movement over it: be it in stealth, in chase
– anything but this standing still or the endless trotting along
narrow tracks.

I take a quick step forwards and with the quicker flash of
teeth from under black lips demand of the fox that we go across.
He can see the excitement in me that I do not try to hide, the
very danger of it to his life if he does not obey. He looks to
the farmhouse and to me once more, and perhaps it is only
because I am the closer hazard that he takes a tentative step out
onto the hillside, away from the trees, his paw sinking deep
into powdery snow.

He moves forwards slowly and after he has gone a few paces
I too leave the trees, stepping out into the pleasant softness,
moving easily and freely down the hill as if it were a hill like
any other, in my home, not to be feared, not an obstacle.
Nervousness tightens my stomach but I am not afraid – I feel
the spring of excitement in my legs and neck yet now it is not
suffocating or holding me back, but a power that I nurse carefully, a strength within me that I control and feel as a young
tree might feel its supple branches bending and swaying in a
gusting breeze.

The slope of the hill ends and we start on the flat of the valley, leaving the thick snow and starting across land trodden firm by the sheep. There is their smell, and that of man as well but faint and much older, and I think that it must be only the pattering of my paws and the fox's that stirs it high enough into the air to reach our noses. I am amazed as I smell it again – I had thought that I would never forget it but even in the time between the last night and this its strangeness is like something new. And yes I am afraid to smell it again, the nervousness in me slithering into something more dangerous, like a snake's tail beneath my paw, but whose long body I am working my way along until I have its head and menace firmly pushed into the ground. I am afraid, but only afraid enough to be alert, to feel the ground rippling out beneath me in every direction.

The fox smells man too and is terrified. His trot ahead of me keeps breaking into a worried lope and then slowing again, his head and ears twitching from side to side. I gouge my paws into the ground for a few strides to bring me up to his side and then with a slight turn and sudden pulse of anger knock him sideways. He calms his skittering trot obediently, slowing to an even pace that I stay level with. Assuaged, my attention turns from the fox to the hill ahead of us, at the top of which resumes the forest, but before both the farmhouse becoming larger up ahead – not in a straight line from our track across the valley but near enough for it to seem suddenly like a lightly sleeping danger.

And then the fox is no longer beside me. He has stopped completely and stands motionless, and turning I stop as well. His eyes have snapped in the direction of the trees at the side of the valley, and he is staring and listening intently, his head quivering as if struggling to catch sight of something he heard. I approach the fox slowly, feeling the beginnings of fear start to lick at me from the cold wind that blows over us. I look to the trees where he gazes but can see nothing. I look back to him and search his body for trickery, for deception in his posture, but his alarm is so close and strong that I cannot believe it to be only his cunning. It must be more than that.

He is still watching the trees, ignoring me next to him, and all I can do is look to where he looks, scanning the dark forms above the paler ground for movement, and then suddenly I catch the awful smell of man as the wind changes – not his dispersed history on the ground but his living warm scent – the smell that makes my heart pound and starts the horrible hot and coldness of fear trickling from my shoulders up into the back of my neck.

The fox smells it too and cowers where he stands as if at a clap of thunder. He looks to me briefly and his eyes are fear and a question: whether I have seen the man. I tell him nothing and instead search the edge of the trees and then all around, turning in tight circles as the fox now does – he and I, together straining our eyes and ears in every direction and sensing nothing but the smell. Then the fox, cringing low on the ground and twisting one way and another as if blustered by a gale, cannot stand it any longer and not caring that he does not know where the man is begins a panicked run as fast as he can towards the other side of the valley. I explode after him, enraged that he is trying to run away, angry at his fear and my own and suddenly wanting nothing more than to sink my teeth into the back of his neck.

I gain quickly on him, bearing down on him easily, feeling the thrill of my greater speed and strength that pulls me towards him and the horrible outcome of this pursuit. What a wonderful feeling to move like this without any doubt but just intent! And the fear – I must have left it behind in the circles I anxiously padded in the snow because again it seems fleeting and unreasonable, for how could man harm me now as I run like this, how could man harm anything gifted with this speed and balance? Nothing could dare come between my will and my actions, not when they are meshed together so closely like this – like a tree to the earth – so closely that when I do catch him the feel of the bite will be inseparable from the first kick into the ground after him.

But something cracks the air – the sound comes sharp and echoing as if from everywhere – and then all is a flash of brightness – everything becomes a hot searing pain that suddenly explodes in my head, a pain unlike any other I have felt, a stabbing, burning agony that lifts me into the air. My body weightless and flailing, my head screaming with furious sensation, I tumble in the light, spinning uncontrollably as if twisted around the torture in my head, not knowing if I am rising or falling until the ground slams into me to take my breath and leave my lying in the snow, shocked – stunned by the terrible burning that rips at my eyes and ears.

I am dying – I must be dying, I think, as I lie here unmoving, feeling nothing but the pain in my head, no cold panic for a stalking death but just the pain itself, drowning all else. I lie still and sense nothing from beyond, as if all that exists is inside me, as if I have been taken from the valley and sunk deep into the cold and dark earth, where at the moment of death I am made to suffer for ever; I am made to suffer in return all the pain I have delivered. Perhaps this is what death is – an endless moment of dying, filled with the agony of the final blow. Do all those that I have killed – do they all still live with my teeth around their throats, with the blood rushing from their stomachs? Am I to exist like this among them, writhing in the earth, feeling nothing but pain and thinking of nothing else than their suffering?

From the darkness and the silence a sound is coming towards me, a regular, pounding noise, and I think for a moment that it is my heart, beating its closing rhythm. But the sound is getting louder, something is coming closer and I realise I listen not from within but to something outside, to a noise coming from the valley, from the living, struggling world where I lie unmoving yet now suddenly and fearfully awake. Footfalls, I realise, coming towards me. Footfalls! – and suddenly my senses are awakened: I see the dark sky above me, the millions of snowflakes falling everywhere endless and without source; I smell man's hated scent, strong and very close and getting stronger as I hear his heavy steps crunching towards me, he the victor, unconcerned, coming to inspect what he has done.

He is almost upon me when without choice I feel my instinct spark to twist my body upright in the snow. My feet placed firmly I push downwards, rising up though my pain to stand suddenly inside it, springing to my feet before the man in an instant and turning sharply to show him my raised and ruined head, surprising him, scaring him, frightening him so that he stumbles backwards and falls over into the snow, the black length of his gun arcing and spinning slowly above and behind him away from his hand.

I turn and begin running for the nearest line of trees, staggering from side to side, moving through a daze of light and pain. I think that I will hear the air crack and be hit again but nothing comes and I am left to stagger onwards, through a space I do not really see but only sense as the ground underneath and long shards of white and yellow pain coming out of the darkness, shards as sharp and hard as ice that I must force my way through to leave the valley and reach the trees.

And once in among them, once deep into the trees' greater darkness away from the valley, I falter to a stop. The pain strikes me like floodwater and I drop to the ground to press my head into the snow, desperate to stop the burning, the torrent of hurt that has me in its grip. I should remain still and let the pain quieten of its own accord but I cannot because I am afraid, I am terrified that this pain will never end and so I writhe in the snow, smearing blood in long and desperate strokes. I still live, but am I to live like this for ever, in this agony? It is not meant to be that I lie here like this – it is not meant to be!

But I become tired, and when I stop moving the cold of the snow begins to soothe the side of my head. My forest has changed, it has become a different place of pain and blindness, but it is still my forest and I find that my breaths are no longer whistling in and out of me, but are lessening, and the ground is cold but exists there beneath me, something I can sense other than my head, something I can push my claws into.

I lie still, and breathe and feel the ground. That is all I do, and I think that after some time I might no longer be awake.

CHAPTER 8

My eye is open, looking up at the tree branches that are beginning to appear, streaking their way across the lightening sky.
With the wounded side of my head pressed into the snow I
think that I cannot move, that I must stay here joined to this
comfort, to the cold that seeps a little way into the pain that
still throbs and pulses like a living thing. It is asleep, the wound
as I lie here, and I worry that if I move I will wake it – I will
wake it and it will burst against me again as it did last night.

How I fear this pain! Even the pain of desperate hunger I
would rather live with for ever, than be forced to cringe again
with every step. I am caught here as I would be by a hunter's
trap, no metal teeth at my leg but still man's intent holding me
down – the ripping and tearing of his gun sticking me fast to
this spot. And, I think, perhaps even being in a trap would be
preferable to this – to this snare of pain and fear where I cannot

put all my anger into the last thrashing snarl as the man approaches, or gnaw through my own leg so that when he comes he will see nothing but a blood-stained stump and be afraid for his world, circled as it is by owners of such will.

But I wonder if I could ever do such a thing. I might lie here and wait, listening to starvation creeping up on me as I would in a trap. But already I begin to know that I won't – I will not be killed by hunger, not after this winter, not after I have struggled my way through its darkest, most lifeless patches and gone days without eating, sometimes thinking that I will never eat again. And besides, there is the fox. The thought of him, of his flattened ears and panicked circles in the snow, makes the branches and sky above me no longer just streaks of differing grey, but the top of the forest, attached to the ground on which I lie – the ground that still holds me so that I do not disappear into the earth.

And somewhere that fox is pacing his way through the trees, perhaps thinking me dead, certainly pleased with his escape. Did he fool me into leading him across the valley, knowing what the man would do? Was the route he showed me a lie, a long and twisting lie designed to make me want to go straight across, all the time him feigning terror of man, knowing that the only way to rid himself of me was to gamble that side-by-side, man's hate of the wolf would be greater?

Anger twists my body upright. The pain rages in my head, but I care more for the hate I can feel surging in me for the fox. Traitorous deceitful creature! To think how I could taste his fear and was fooled into thinking it real! But I will not make that mistake again. He will probably beg, he will plead and appeal to my stomach and I will be tempted, but this time I will not listen. All I will do is find him and kill him.

I find that I can get up, that my legs, though shaking, obey enough to lift me to standing. My head shakes as well, a looseness from my neck as if it is slipping around on the smell of my own blood that rises from beneath me. The pain is there, but becoming mixed with anger, waking me, sharpening my senses, and I am proud, strangely proud of the sudden desire I have to kill.

And so I move off, tracking along the high edge of the valley, each footfall flaring in my head so that I shudder as I step. But now I am pushed on by anger and the pain must become just another thing to which I must adapt. My movement changes: I barely lift my paws from the snow but skim them through its surface so they do not have to drop too far to the ground. After a while I am stepping so lightly that the pain is steadied and I am almost tempted to feel that its threat has passed. But when I stagger, or when the snow is deceptive and my paw falls deep into it to jolt me, the pain yelps inside my head and I must pause, waiting for it to fade. In this way I keep moving and looking, smelling the ground and moving on again, pausing less now as the pain becomes more bearable. And I notice that the greys of dawn around me are becoming coloured with red.

It does not seem to take long and the light is only a little stronger when I stumble across the fox's scent, lying low over the ground, richly sour with fear and exhaustion. Smelling it, my heart beats harder, the pain in my head flares and then lessens. I am happy to have found the trail so easily, as I thought perhaps I might not be able to after the damage of last night. But it is only a single patter of happiness, which does nothing to wash away my anger, and I follow the scent intently as it weaves through and under the broken trees, the light of dawn becoming stronger, turning everything a pink-tinged grey – a strange brightness I have often relished, yet one that now seems pointless.

Then ahead not far away I see what must be him: a patch of red-brown fur on the pink-tinted snow, a small mound unmoving and asleep, unaware of my approach that slows to a silent and careful walk. He lies curled at the edge of a glade, dwarfed by the tree at the base of which he lies, his snout tucked firmly among the tangle of his paws and tail for warmth – and I step silently into the clearing towards him, the trees at my side surrounding me as I approach him in the soft red light.

Yet I must make a noise, for suddenly his small head swivels upwards, his eyes slits but his ears pricked, and when he sees me it is as if his whole body sinks into the snow, his eyes widened, his neck tense and held low and tilted to one side in submission.

I should be killing him now, not standing here in sudden indecision! But the anger that I held so clearly for him is suddenly muddied inside of me, like the blood in my body that I can feel leaking into parts it shouldn't. Perhaps it is the angle of his neck, the command of another like me not to strike – or is it just the pitiful smallness of his body when compared to the base of the tree behind it? Whatever it is it has stopped me, and like him I tilt my head, not in submission but to hide my wound, the wound that has robbed me of an eye, for where there should be the red and glowing forest there is now only a shifting brightness out of which appears no structure or shape.

But with my remaining eye I see the fox, who trembles still half-curled in the snow, waiting quietly and watching me with fear and downcast eyes, no sign of fight remaining in his small red-brown frame. His eyes flit over my body with a flash of disbelief, as if they see the dawn's mist suddenly made alive and real in the form before them. He cannot look me in the eye and seems only able to look at the cold air around me, his eyes shifting and darting, his head trembling low over the pale pink snow. Then slowly his eyes follow the line of my foreleg up to my chest, creeping so slowly that he might be examining every hair of the fur on my neck. I find that I angle my head further as his eyes are about to reach my own. I don't know why I do this. That I do makes me suddenly afraid.

His eye makes contact with mine and immediately he is pleading with me, showing me the farmhouse as it was when we stood at the top of the hill looking downwards, his fear of

84

crossing the valley and again, the long twisting path he wanted to take to go around it. To show me these lies again! I can feel anger burning in my shoulders as I take another step towards him. He cringes even lower and I stare at each of his eyes, searching for the next thoughts from them, hungry to see what rage they will trigger in my own.

And perhaps if he had shown me the long route again, or even if he had challenged me or snarled at my wish to go straight across, I might have hesitated further – but his eyes show nothing but pleading and a desperate request for mercy, the same look I have seen in all of them and I am helpless to do anything but lunge forwards with fury, angling my neck to aim at the back of the fox's head, the pain in my head thudding deeply with the sudden movement but still wanting nothing more than to get there and keep biting until I feel my teeth touching each other through the thin bones and flesh of his skull. But as I open my jaws to grip the fox the pain of my wound increases, emerging through my anger like a rising scream, turning my blood to ice with fear of its terrible return and then exploding in my head with a new and impossible agony as I try to bite. It is worse, the pain, than when it first came – there is no shock to numb it – I felt it coming as I opened my jaws and now it has me in its grip and I am reeling away from the fox, dazed, my eye clamped shut, swaying where I stand.

I still myself and wait for the pain to subside, fighting the panic that it will never end, pushing away the fear that I must die and will die now in agony. It is as if only I remain, standing here feeling nothing except the pain in my head while everything passes on, everything but nothing I care for, all else unreal and distant beyond the agony of this moment. But slowly, so slowly that at first it is more of a hope than a feeling, the pain begins to recede and as it trickles away relief begins to grow in me like a bloom, cautious as if in late winter, tentative, as if afraid of some returning enemy but growing all the time until I know for sure that the pain is going and I am spared. The cold feeling of the snow beneath my paws returns, and the quiet sounds of the forest make their way through a haze of relief so that I remember where I am and what has just happened. My sole eye is still closed, but I open it slowly, and from the blur of sudden brightness I see a swathe of red-brown that clears into the shape of the fox standing before me, his small head held low, his eyes wide and aghast with incomprehension.

I have been standing unbalanced and stagger towards him. He shrinks back a few steps, and I see that he is afraid of me – unsure, but afraid nonetheless. He is staring at the wounded mess at the side of my head and so I step forwards, turning my head away so that the injury is masked and instead my eye is revealed, stabbing down at him as he cowers.

What does he see in me now? Does he see the fear and confusion I hold for the pain that stopped me from biting? Or does he see what I suddenly grasp at, what I want him to see – the swan – larger and more glorious in my mind than it ever was in his? He must see the swan because now I can see it in his eyes too, he is feeding my thoughts with his own, showing me the curve of muscular wing, the mass of flesh under the snow of soft white feathers. My stomach coils with the prospect like a lizard's tail, and as it does so I am not so afraid – and the more I think of the swan the more I can see myself growing before the fox, becoming stronger and more dangerous in his eyes, his own uncertainty of my power wiped away by my sudden desire.

And although it might be nothing more than the fox's lie I find myself thinking now only of the swan and how if I find it, it might end it all. What is this winter, where crows will hunt foxes and wolves cannot bite? I have looked away from the fox for an instant but now I return to his small eyes and command him to lead. Obeying, he turns and begins to walk away slowly, looking back once to see if I follow, then continuing faster when he sees that I am.

CHAPTER 9

Following the fox, I trot lightly behind him and watch as the land begins to change – the trees start to thin and the ground moves upwards, gently at first and then steeper until we are forced to slow to a fast walk. The trees become scattered and we move through one clearing to the next, while ahead and rising above it all I see the vague mounds of hills and behind them, dark and massive, the clear shape of distant mountains.

As we move the pain in my head throbs with each step, reminding me of my injury, filling me with sudden risings of cold panic at how I had tried to kill the fox only to find that my jaws were useless. I wonder if the pain will ever stop, if my lust will return to the tips of my teeth and I will look back with shame to this moment. Perhaps I will be half-draped over another brought down, my belly in their entrails spread across the warm ground of a summer's evening, pulling at the soft meat of their rump, and I will remember this walk behind the fox – the weakness of the thoughts I had, the foolish worry that I would never kill again.

The ground begins to rise steeply and as I am reduced to pushing each paw with great effort into the snow I feel the onset of a horrible coldness. Moving like this I should not feel cold. But it is not my body that is cold. I may dream of lying next to another that I have brought down, another whose neck I have slashed open, but the vision is hollow – this coldness I can feel is from within me, it is my terror at a permanent and unwanted change, it is the scraping ice of change itself, the passing of a thing into something else that whispers to me that I might never return to what I was before.

My legs numb and stiff, tired by the trudging climb, my step begins to falter, each lifting of a heavy paw a separate and difficult event, the fatigue of my body weighing me down like stone. Tiredness I have known, but now beneath the sluggishness of my muscles there is a different weakness – one that is draining not only my strength but my will. Where before it has always screamed inside of me, a simple emptiness demanding to be filled, now for the first time I wonder at the need to push on, to keep moving. I have become blind in one eye but lost the blindness to exhaustion and the emptiness of fruitless pursuit – the thing I imagine every breathing creature in the forest fears of the wolf. Never have I found myself dreading each step, fearing every repetitive lift and push into the snow, hoping for any escape from this pointless exertion. I lift a paw to take another step, but suddenly all reason to drops away and I feel as if I am falling, but I have only stopped – willingly I stop, and the fox must hear the silence from behind as he too has stopped walking and turned to look.

I command of him that we take a rest. He seems to consent, his eyes saying nothing, his stance neutral, and I wait for him to lie in the snow first before stiffly I lower myself from standing. We face each other, small fox and injured wolf, he watching me warily and with a strange curiosity while I stare back, the wound in my head throbbing intensely, the unbearable heaviness of exhaustion washing into my relaxing muscles in a sudden flood.

Why does he look at me in that way, I wonder. He seems to watch me with patient interest, as if he waits for something not with dread but with expectancy, with a hopeful eagerness that he tries to mask in his eyes. If I did not know him to be afraid of me I would think there was the flash of the predator across those stones in his head – the light I have seen in my own kind when they have seen something and are calling me to the hunt, or just the reflection of something struggling in their eyes.

Is he looking at me and seeing a creature struggling, a creature clinging onto its life?

Surely he does not see me in this way! He is still afraid – that is clear – I can smell it and see it in the rest of his thoughts. But there is that glimmer of hope within his fear, and I am afraid to accept what it might mean, what it is he has seen in me. A chilling desperation surrounds me like the cold air, cloying and inescapable and reducing my breaths to shallow pants. I am afraid to think about any of it: of my wound, of this winter, of the shock of finding the fox beneath those crows. But while there is the swan there is prospect, and though I feel a great falseness within me I look to the fox and ask him of it, how he knows of it, feeling hope shimmer in me like the illusion of a distant heat, like the brightness of the sun in the bitter cold.

His eyes widen with the flash of menace, the glint of deception as if about to convey a lie, and I feel my hope slipping away to nothing. Then I see the swan in his mind and I cannot doubt that once he saw it, that once, even, he was close to it. Perhaps he shows me this because he knows that the swan is becoming my only hope – he sees death creeping towards me but is still afraid of the danger I pose. I watch him with a single eye, demanding more, a snarl seeping out from my throat towards him. I realise that I might be begging but I don't care – the more I think of the swan the more I think it might change all of this. This winter has been strange enough that he might lead me to it and if such a thing happens maybe my wound will heal; it will mend itself like other wounds I have had and I will be restored, I will return to what I was, no longer weak, to prey instead on the weak!

And perhaps it is only more cunning for his own protection that makes the fox show me the swan again. He is guarding his thoughts, only showing me darkened glimpses. But what is this? Where before I had thought he had buried the swan, now there is no sign of this in his mind. He is showing me the swan and it is not buried but standing tall, shining as white as the snow, one of its great wings spread across the ground, damaged. Does this mean that the bird is still alive, that it is not buried, but flightless is trapped? If so why would he have not already killed it? Perhaps he has killed it and will only lead me to some putrid remains, the last few buried bones with his teeth marks all over them. I look at him – his small frame of skin and tendon lying there with all the strength of a pile of rotting leaves – and suddenly I feel hope pool in my chest, because I look at him and realise that he does not have the power to kill such a bird – he is too small! The bird, though flightless, could still break him in two with a swipe from the wing it still holds against its side. Perhaps he is leading me to it because he hopes that I will kill it for him – and in return for leading me to it he thinks I will let him have his fill!

He stares at me levelly, his eyes firm and unwavering. I am begging for him to show me more, trying to suck it out from his green eyes, and the fox, knowing this, seeing that I would rather have more knowledge of the swan than the return of spring itself, cruelly turns away to deprive me.

I feel rage pulsating in me, coursing around my jaws that I would, if able, plunge into the smaller animal before me. I am burning in my own weakness, wanting nothing more than to thrash everything around me into bloody shreds. The fox must sense this, as I see that his next breath goes in deeper, his chest expanding and his head rising a little higher. Yet he does not realise that when he looks back, when he turns back, the victor of this contest, his guard has dropped and I see suddenly what he tries to hide – I see like a flash his memory of the white shape fluttering into the side of a rock face, of it falling downwards and tumbling before disappearing somewhere into the grey rock. And then a red-brown shape that he watched with concern, scrambling up the rock in pursuit of the bird, lost from sight as he nervously paced below looking upwards after it.

The fox, seeing that he has revealed more than he wanted, becomes downcast, his eyes misting over like the ice of a puddle, nothing beneath them but a murky darkness, neither shallow nor deep. I look away from him to the trees and the snow and the trees beyond, their black spikes emerging from the white ground in a thick mass that from here has no visible end.

I look away because I do not want him to see that I am hopeful – I do not want the fox to see that though my instinct softly warns for caution in my desperation I am suddenly elated with prospect, for I saw and can still see now what the fox had seen, how the bird, white and brilliant and arcing though the air, had then tilted into the rock face to tumble and disappear.

But what of the red-brown shape moving up the rock, scrambling towards where the bird disappeared? And the fox – he had paced below with fear, watching the shape rise upwards to become smaller and vanish. He did not want me to see that, but why? I should be suspicious – yet the vision of the bird seen in the fox's thoughts, crashing and tumbling against the rock, it is too much like the excitement of a hunt beginning, like the crash of hooves, the burst of movement that can only ever pull me forwards.

I push upwards into standing and the fox stands with me, him a little wary, worried by the new energy he must sense in me. I am afraid of the pain but I step quickly towards him, not turning my head, letting him see the wound that I imagine must shine like the sun to his eyes, as brightly as it hurts me. He

shrinks back, his eyes still frosted over, but in the movement of his legs and paws is the speed of fear, of disgust, and he knows that I want him to lead, for him to take me to the swan, and I see in him an instant of anger, before he becomes meek again and turns slowly to move off.

We have rested long and already travelled far; the light is beginning to fade and is only the dimness of a winter afternoon – the permanent gloom not brought by cloud but by the onset of a short day's end. The land continues to rise upwards, the trees no longer in clumps surrounding clearings but thinning overall until there is more open space than trees, and here, where the wind whips viciously down and across us over the open snow, the trees are suddenly replaced by rocks and boulders whose sharp sides jut dark and grey from beneath the

97

white covering. Looking at the fox I see his small body plodding ahead, the only patch of colour against the white of the ground and the grey of the sky and the darker grey of the mountains beyond – the mountains not near but no longer distant, their unavoidable form huge and through the dimness intensely clear.

We walk towards these monuments, but they are more than a day away and we get no closer or they bigger. Instead we begin to clamber through the foothills – smooth mounds of snow-coloured rock that undulate from beneath our feet, rolling away and upwards to meet the distant mountains, waves of white punctured by the pointed shapes of a million boulders. But ahead, near and lying across the whole length of the horizon, I see a wall of rock rising starkly up from the ground, a grey cliff face that separates the land into high and low, as if the part I walk on has slumped downwards, the steep bank of stone the place at which it was cut.

The fox is also staring at the cliff face, and perhaps sensing me watching him he turns as he walks – in his eyes a mixture of fear and satisfaction, a look in which the scar of rock cutting across the land is given a huge significance. I think that we must be nearing our destination and my chest tightens with excitement. For a moment the pain in my body lifts and I become sharply aware of my surroundings, of the strangeness of this land and having left the forest I know so well behind me. And whereas in the forest I love the gloom of late in a winter's day, here – where rocks have replaced the trees and the wind slashes across the ground between them – here the gloom carries only menace.

CHAPTER 10

It is almost night and we still have not reached the cliff. I don't look up to see if the stars are out, or even if the sky is clear, because I am too tired to look upwards. The evening falls stealthily as I look at the ground in front of me, at the little prints made by the fox on the snow that has steadily darkened. Night should excite me – filled with prospect it has always excited me – but this night seems to only promise the certainty of further struggle, and I find myself suddenly desperate to lie down and sleep.

Moving along, I listen to the fox's paws pushing into the snow, the sound of which has become like a second heartbeat, the empty space of snow and rock being otherwise so quiet around us. It seems like such an easy sound and I find myself looking up, hating his movement as he walks ahead, him unimpaired and without another's tracks to walk within while

I, injured, must stagger to keep up. Then the soft padding of his paws stops and I look up from the snow to see his small shape halted before me, gloomy in the dusk, a vague hint of colour behind which the dark grey expanse of the rock face rises suddenly and hugely behind him. He is turned away from me, and slowing gratefully I approach, the thought of resting for a while beginning to swim and clamour in my back and legs.

We stand together at the base of the cliff, the wind gentle and not the carrier of the intense coldness that is here, that seems to be seeping out of the wall of rock itself. I peer at the cliff and its blank, flat side – how it rises higher than many a tree's height, and as I look at it I realise that this must be where the swan is, this is the place where, at least, the fox saw it and was therefore able to show it to me, tumbling in the air and disappearing. Was it attacked by man as I have been? Is that what could bring it down from the air and into this place?

Now the fox turns to face me and I ask of him if this is the place where he saw the swan. I had expected him to not answer, at least not without diversion, because I am afraid that he is beginning to see how desperate I am for the reality of this search. But he does not choose to deny me the answer, or even make me wait – his eyes are simple in their assent and in them I can see the bird again, powerful, brilliant white in the darkness and turning towards me so that I am entranced, hunger filling my stomach and pushing drool out between my teeth, the blood in my chest and dripping down from my head feeling like the heat of fire.

This is not a lie. The fox shows me this with such clarity that I feel I could step into his thoughts and the swan would be there before me. Even he, clever as he is, could not merely show me that to deceive me – I can see in him that this swan is still alive, and nearby, and for a moment he and I are truly joined as predators, we allow ourselves to share in the lust we have for this bird's flesh, the desire to crush the life from its head and take the power from its wings into our own bodies. Yes, it must be close! In the same way a beast can sense danger when you have made no fault in your approach, now I can sense this swan. Its presence seems to hum from the rock face like the cold, aching with life, pushing out towards the heat of my blood.

I look up to the cliff and its impassive face. I can see no feature, no ledge or detail sticking out from it and think that maybe if I had the use of both eyes I might, but not for certain.

My eye falls back to the fox and instantly he changes – there is some of the fire we shared for the swan still flickering in his eyes but beneath that a sudden, shocking lack of fear for me. I am frightened as I watch his teeth appear and his shoulder lowering, not of the sharpness of his jaws which are flying towards me but for the desperation in his intent because I understand it – I understand him and how he is moving now in a place where his mind has dropped like a stone into his instinct and bound him to act. I have seen it in the eyes of others – I have felt it in myself – and so I recoil away from the fox as if he were a dangerous snake, turning slightly to prepare for his bite and watch as triumph glistens in his eyes as he does not attack me but pushes back into the ground, turning quickly to begin streaking down away from me along the rock's base.

For a moment I am paralysed. I should be exploding after him, but for an instant I am filled with doubt: I don't know why it is that I should chase him again, or what I will do when I have caught up with him – and would it not be better to just lie here and sleep, maybe awakening to a clearer world? My legs feel like stone and my back like a rotten bough. But lie down now and I might never get back up. I am being pursued by something that might take me in my sleep, and suddenly as I watch the fox diminishing I realise he may already be too far away. And the presence of the swan – the wonderful pulsating heat I felt even in this bleak place and its coldness – that presence is going away too, as if it flies above the fox and he is its shadow. I could let him go easily – I am so exhausted I might let a hare run beneath me, but I cannot let him take the swan with him, not in this winter, not wounded like this as I am.

I feel my body sink into my feet, my paws splaying over as much snow as the fox's corpse will cover and then the sudden lurching forwards from this grip, the air stinging my eye as my legs stretch to their full gallop. I am gaining on the fox – rapidly – he is no match for my greater speed. Then he seems to slow almost to a stop and for a moment I think that he has given up and will return to the quivering submission of before. But he does not stop completely – instead he turns and suddenly leaps onto the rock, scrambling upwards to a small ledge, and just as I slide and turn beneath him in the snow he leaps to another ledge and then another, carefully and accurately making his way up the sheer cliff face.

I watch him rise above me and for an instant I think that the chase must end. Then I see the first ledge to which he leapt, and after scraping my way up onto it I can see the next and I follow him upwards hesitantly, only seeing the next ledge of the route after landing on the previous, while the fox – he knows it well, it seems, because he is far quicker and leaving me behind. Each time I reach the next ledge I look up to see where he is and each time he is higher and smaller.

I follow, determined, leaping from ledge to ledge, my legs weakening and my nerve at every jump threatening to snap. The ledges of the route up this cliff are becoming more difficult to spot in the fading light and as I face another distant target of level rock and sink down onto my hind legs I can feel how the strength is leaking from them, how the next push up into the air might not be enough. The next ledge I miss with one paw and for a moment think that I will fall. I manage to cling on – the paw that was in the air finds something beneath it and I scrabble my way onto the ledge. Shaken, my heart pounding and my legs singing with fatigue, I stop to rest. I stand for a long time, breathing deeply and my eye closing with the weight of exhaustion, knowing that I should move on but unable to find the will.

The remaining light is almost my imagination, and when the last of it trickles away into darkness the rock of the cliff face becomes a featureless swathe of grey and black with no ledge or path visible among it. The ledge that I stand on is so narrow that my paws are pressed together and I lean into the rock at my side, afraid that if I don't the rising wind will take hold and pull me down onto the dark ground far below. I am afraid to be on this ledge now, but I realise with a rising horror that I cannot go forwards as a leap from here would be onto nothing but dark air. I try shuffling backwards on the ledge, thinking that there might be more room to turn around and make my way back down, but as I edge backwards my rearmost paw slips and is suddenly unsupported.

I am stuck. I am stuck and will have to stand here like this, pressed against rock that feels like it is trying to push me away. As night deepens it brings more snow and a wind that sends the falling flakes spiralling and dipping in violent whirls against the cliff face. I stand on the tiny ledge, clinging desperately, buffeted and whipped by the snow that stings my eye where sight remains. Cold and tired, my legs begin to tremble and my paws, wide though they are, begin to slip beneath me.

Suddenly I am not afraid. With my eye closed and the wind rushing up against my side I may already be falling. Perhaps if I have slipped and am to die the coming earth will end the sadness I feel – a sadness not for my death but for the moment of dying, the moment where the ever-useless struggle ends; where in revelation all fight and suffering are proved worthless. I have seen, chased and torn the creatures that would save themselves, and now I am the wretched – the sufferer on this thin ledge waiting for death, life leaking from my wounded head and pooling thickly in my crippled jaw. I am saddened, and I see that I have brought them down and killed them and ripped them open always amongst this sadness, yet hiding it with snarls and flashing teeth and anger for their pitiable efforts.

The night flows around me with wind and cold and the rock at my side, trying to push me off the ledge. My paws keep slipping and as I try to grip on the stone it feels that any purchase will bounce me off the rock, malignant at my flank. I am helpless! I am like the staggering and wet newborn calf whom I hate as I hate myself now, trembling on thin legs upon this ledge in weakness. And in my mind I can feel a tearing, as if something long trapped is now using its teeth to free itself, and I shut my eye to escape it. I clench my eye tightly but now I see it more clearly, I see them clearly, each one changing into another stronger than the last, their spinning legs and tails and the dust their hooves have raised, the slips in the snow, the lowered horns, the manic jumps and their eyes all alike, all in the end alike to the calf – the stupid brutal innocence of the calf.

What was I? I do not know what it was that walked over the warming earth only to be stopped suddenly by a bright smell, a stench that had me diving into the forest with a quickened heart and the sickness in my stomach raging into my head. And then to jump over a rotting stump as I went, only for the stump to move beneath a paw that brushed it, a strange feeling as if the earth and everything on it had moved a fraction as I leapt. But when I landed – when I landed in the long grass and bent to sniff at the wetness on my paw to find the same smell that had me running in the first place, I could do nothing but slowly make my way back. I pushed through the grass, the green edges flicking at my nose and teeth and slicing my tongue, and then there it was, a calf, steam rising from its wet hide, its ears bent and squashed by birth, its head tottering on its neck as it turned to look at me.

I remember the trees of that place, the patches of grass, the way the ground curved around the roots and the places I slept in because I did not have to leave it for days. As I walked towards the calf I did not yet know that its mother was dead a little beyond it. I was wary for her appearance but knew silently that she was dead, that the calf and I were alone. And as I got closer it tried to stand. Its legs pushed and flailed at the ground and then it was on the joints of its forelegs, shaking, its ears dripping and its chest heaving with fear and effort. I stopped and watched. I drank the movements, the smells and the sounds of it trying to stand as I would the water of a thin but deep stream in summer. It fought desperately to stand and long enough for most of the wetness to have dried from its back – and when the last leg was pushing upwards away from the ground and a simple hope flashed through its eye I streaked forwards and took it through the neck, crouching down to hit it upwards, a perfect kill, the most perfect of kills, the calf dead before we both landed softly into the grass behind it.

And now I am the calf – I am trapped by circumstance as it was by nature. I am ashamed for that calf. I am ashamed for us both – that we must ever be made to feel helpless!

But from this night eventually comes the light of day and soon the sky is grey enough that I can see the form of the rock on which I stand, a dark line running up to my paw and turning beneath its claws into the cliff. Exhausted, my legs and body trembling and pained from remaining still for so long, I begin to peer forwards and upwards, searching for the next ledge. I strain my neck out, slipping on the thin ledge made wet and icy by the melting heat of my paws, wondering perhaps if the path goes downwards as well as up. Just below I can see what looks to be the lip of a rock jutting out, and with a sudden flicker of hope I crane forwards to see it better. But as I do so my forepaw slips from the ledge and while I try desperately to lean back against the rock suddenly I am pitching forwards as if thrown – my body is tumbling over the ledge and I am falling, twisting in mid air and all I can think is that now, surely, I will die.

I do not feel the ground beneath rising up to hit me – instead I half land on the lip of rock below – my hind legs are thrashing at the air but my head and the front half of my body is gripping desperately to the cliff face – my claws are slipping on the rock but by pulling with them and twisting my neck and my head and pushing and scrabbling with my hind legs I am able to scramble onto the rock. This ledge is wider, a lake of space compared to the last, and I plunge into it – I feel something hard beneath every paw, beneath my tail, beneath the length of my legs and my chest and finally my jaw as I lower myself to lying, breaths of panic pushing red foam from my nostrils. My eye closes, the light of morning is forced away and I am falling again but into sleep, and I think with the slightest glimmer that if I am to be taken – if I am to be taken now I will lead the way.

CHAPTER II

When I wake up I am confused, wondering why I wake up to pain in my chest and head, and why the ground beneath me is so hard. Then I remember landing on the lip of rock and the scraping, desperate climb onto it. I open a single eye and remember more, all of it suddenly coming out of the cloudiness of sleep, and as it does my heart sinks in my chest like something thrown, sending out ripples of shame and helplessness into the rest of my body. I lie motionless for a while and then stand and stretch slowly, my whole body sore with fatigue and the pain in my head starting again to pound unbearably with the smallest movement.

The light of day is still strong. I look to the sky and the part of it that I can see against the grey of the cliff is white with small patches of blue, while beneath it runs the open white rocky fields of this place up to where the trees begin again – isolated tiny groups of them at first and then the silent darker white mass together and covering all of it into the distance. I have never seen the forest from this high up – I always felt the forest to be never-ending but to see it now stretching away is a torture, is to be shown the greatness of something at the moment of it being taken away. I can see my home, yet I can't smell or hear it or feel it beneath me! I want to be back there, among the trees, not here perched like a bird on this land's claw of rock.

The platform that I am on is large – I turn around without fear of falling and see it stretching back into the cliff, tapering as it does and ending in a black patch in the stone. My chest tightens and my breathing stops. I raise my head higher and it stabs at me with the movement, but I do not care because I peer at this patch – this dark smudge that might just be a darker shade of rock, or a trick of the light on my eye, but that my now feral hope snarls at me to be the entrance of a cave.

I begin to breathe again and drop my head to the rock base on which I stand, sucking the air in and smelling my own blood, the blank scent of the rock and, crouched among it, as if hiding, the scent of the fox. He has been here! I walk forwards with my head down towards the black patch, my eye fixed on it and willing it to form into the opening I crave, following the fox's trickling scent that can only be going in a straight path towards the hole ahead. Quickly I look up and around, searching for another route, but the walls of stone are sheer – there can be no other way off this ledge but the fall to the ground behind me.

And a few paces later I see it is no trick of the light, but a hole – a crack in the rock that recedes into darkness – and I stand before it, the daylight brightening behind me with something near to sunlight and making the black of the opening thicker. I sniff at the base of the hole. The fox has been through here, through this hole for certain – his smell is faint but lurid among my senses – and I wonder where he may have gone and what is beyond, whether what is hidden as my only hope within this mountain is the swan that he told me of, or just his weak stench left like deception. Lowering my neck I peer into the darkness, smelling strange scents that mix confusingly, seeing with one eye only a blur of black and grey and hearing no sound except what sounds like dripping water, a quiet and steady rhythm echoing weakly as if distant.

The crack is small and I have to crawl into it on my belly, the hard rock beneath scraping painfully against my bruised chest. I push forwards, seeing nothing in the sudden darkness until the fissure seems to widen and I try to stand, feeling the roof of the cave on my shoulders and back and its base beneath my feet, shuffling forwards like this blindly until the rock finally lifts from above and I am almost standing unburdened. It is too dark for me to see anything and I begin to worry that it will be permanently dark here, but as I edge further in more light follows me and my eye adjusts – soon I can make out the sharp lines of rock and structure around me, seeing how the cave's ceiling widens as it burrows into the mountain, its furthest end lost in darkness. Looking to my paws I find that I am standing on a wide ledge, still so close to the cave's ceiling that I have to stoop, while below me and cut deeply into the rock is a hole filled with water – a black pool of stagnant liquid from which the smells of filth and waste rise together thick and choking.

The pool is large and its rear is lost in the same darkness as the ceiling, but in its centre is a small rock poking from the oily surface, rounded and smeared with paler streaks that cover it almost entirely. I see no swan, yet I can smell among the stench of rotting and soiled water what might be its scent – yet perhaps like the fox it was here once but isn't now, and I think with the bitter loss of all hope that perhaps I smell its rotting corpse.

I am about to turn and leave the stench of the cave when I see a flicker of movement quiver from the darkness at the far end of the pool. I hold my head perfectly still, fearing that my single eye tricks me, yet willing it to bore into the black swathe of darkness, not with hope but with the certainty of desperation, expecting nothing yet knowing there is something there – that there must be something there. I wait but nothing moves, and while I fear it was just the movement of my head that made me see something, I *know* there is something there for I can hear the faint sound of something whispering between the drips of water.

My eye wide and staring, I tilt my head from side to side, trying to catch again the tremble I saw, listening to the faintest of sounds that would vanish instantly if I did not hold on to them with all my attention. Slowly I move to the ledge's end, keeping my head as still as possible, straining with all my senses to reach into the darkness that spreads before me. My paws on the edge, I lean forwards, stretching my neck and head out above the pool, blood falling from my wound to drip suddenly into the water below and smashing into the sounds I had been desperately trying to capture. Then I feel something move and slither beneath my paw, smooth and cold like a stone – a moment later a loud splash erupts from beneath, making me flinch and echoing shockingly around the cave.

And in the darkness something moves again and this time I see it unmistakably: a large shape pressed up against the far wall of the sunken pool, flattened against the rock as if trying to disappear into it, stretching up and then slipping down against its sheer and unclimbable face. I freeze and can do nothing but stare, senseless and without feeling, seeing the clear shape of a wing emerge and the flame-like lick of a neck pressed against the rock. It is the swan, I know, but not the swan I had imagined, not the swan that was the sum of all my hope, but instead a desperate and trembling creature, grey and cowering, a tattered and grazed body floating on the scum of black oily water, moving with only the merest hint of life.

The flame of its long neck quivers and turns, and even though it is dark – even though the space before me is nothing but shades of darkness – I see the glistening of its small eye – a tiny speck of vibrancy shining silently, as if able to gather all the meagre light of the cave and strike it back towards me. What an eye this is that holds me! There is none of the defiance of the beast, none of the begging of hare or fox. Instead there is a depth, a blackness not like the water of a pool but like a moonless, starless sky, and instantly I know that the swan has seen me and understood – it knows how I came here to take its life but am wounded, weakened – that I cannot kill by bite but may still by holding it beneath the oily surface of the water. It sees this and is unafraid. It pushes away from the far wall of the pool, its body revolving smoothly beneath its still head so that both are matched in my direction and for a moment in the double curl of its frayed wings I see the undoubted grace of its nature – a painful sight – a beautiful thing but only for those still seeing through a hunter's eye, which I no longer do.

It drifts closer on the water and I feel my back legs twitch with anticipation. A dull anger throbs at my ears and I think that I will jump at it and risk the blows of its wings, feel the slicking grip of the water around my eye as I take it down to the bottom of the pool with me. Yet we both stop. The swan must see something of my intent because it stops and retreats a little, but inside of me something has stopped as well – the will I had to smother the bird has left, disappeared: the thought of swallowing, of drowning in the foul liquid that sticks in my nostrils and throat like quills, is suddenly too strong to release my legs and send me forwards.

And in the swan's eyes there is a warning. As soon as it tilts its head I see myself: I am standing on the stained rock in the centre of the pool, my back curved and my neck low, my fur covered with the filth of the water. I am growling and trembling and watching as something moves around me, lashing out and losing my grip on the grime-covered stone to slip forwards and send my chest and head slumping into the pool. I watch myself thrashing in the water, trying to turn around and get back onto the rock, and watching this I become afraid, because I understand how I might do this until the end of my life if I go into the pool after the swan – how it could easily circle around me and keep out of reach of my desperate efforts until eventually I drown with exhaustion, or die of starvation after hauling myself back onto the rock for the last time, nothing but breathless skin and bone, draped over it another streak of grey.

But how is it that the swan can see this? It shows me these things with the clarity of something seen, as if it has already watched me standing and snarling on the rock, striking out at it and flying into the pool, only to have to return after fruitless paddling in the stinking water. And then I begin to understand, because through its eyes it is showing me how the fox was standing in almost complete darkness – I see the bird guiding its body that is willing and meek, nudging its paws with its long neck and beak, angling its body with silent pressures. I see how the fox leapt forwards and disappeared into a tunnel above, a jump made blindly in darkness, a leap made almost daily and in return for the swan's guidance the scraps of food, dropped into the oily water for the bird to gobble gratefully – a cycle of parent and young made between predator and prey, a perversion that shocks me and that I do not understand, but revealed so quickly and with such stark clarity that I cannot doubt it.

But in the length of a breath I do begin to doubt. I wonder if the swan – a creature unknown to me – has some trick or ability in deception that it is using to save itself. Looking down into the pool, it seems certain with its high sheer walls that to enter it once would mean there would be no way to leave by the way I came. And the swan – it too is trapped. Why, if it could possibly leave, would it choose to stay here? By the filth and stench from the cave it has been here a long time, and yet there is no other life in here, nothing, not even the simple green slime that covers rocks near water. It must get its food from the fox – maybe it uses the same ability in deception to force the fox to return each day and drop the bundle from its mouth into the water.

Inside me I feel the quiet pulse of realisation, as if I had lost the trail of some small animal only to realise suddenly that it is hidden under a nearby stone. I turn in the gloom and begin to make my way back to the opening, having to lower myself and squeeze again through the sharp stone until my nose is in sunlight and then all of me is standing again in cold fresh air, free of the stench of the cave. But, searching the rock plat-form, I am disheartened – I had expected to look again and see something I missed, see the route by which the fox gets away from the cave, but there is no route! I pace back and forwards along the ledge, looking in every direction, cocking my head and thinking that perhaps I don't see it because of the loss of one eye. But there is no way to get off this platform except by falling over the edge and to the ground.

I stand at the precipice, looking down at the snow beneath and wonder if I could possibly survive the leap. I know I never could but am so desperate that I allow myself the weakness to think for a moment that I might – and then I am ashamed. There is no fox's corpse there either, none dashed on the rocks that jut out below, and yet his smell is on the stone that I stand on, in the opening to the cave and in the cave itself. The swan must show the truth! If I am to get off this rock – this hard lifeless thing beneath my paws that now I find I hate – I will have to enter that pool and somehow find the way by which the fox escapes.

But the thought of that water around me, spilling into my mouth and nose and clinging at my sides, seems worse than anything, worse even than man, and wipes away the last of my hope to leave me empty – a space quickly filled by a sudden and desperate yearning for my home. Then fatigue and dull pain return to my body and I stand motionless as they come, looking out over the expanse of whiteness below and longing for the trees of the forest, to smell the scents of wood and earth.

Turning away from the edge I stagger and realise that my body is weakening further from my wound. Encountering the swan, the deception or otherwise in its eyes and the hope it gave me pushed away these things, but now I fear I might be in the final weakening: a drowsy lightness in the head that softens everything: sights, smells – for a moment even the rock feels soft beneath my paws. But I still stand and have not fallen yet. If I were back down on the ground instead of trapped up here I feel I could run as fast and for as long as I ever have! I would put my head up and bend my back to eat up the ground beneath, not stopping until deep in the forest!

Because if I am to die it must be there – it must be there and not here in this harsh and alien place.

Resolved, I pace back to the hole and dive through into the dark and foul-smelling cave. I scramble quickly forwards then stop because my eye has not adjusted to the dark, and when it does I see that the swan does not seem to have moved but still floats in the same position, perhaps knowing that I could only return. Anger is in my shoulders and throbbing at my head and again I feel the urge to fling myself at it, to get my forelegs and neck clamped around its weak neck and pull it down to the bottom of the pool. How long would we sink like that? Is the pool so deep that we would die thrashing and twisting around each other before we hit the bottom? I know that the swan sees these thoughts in me because I make no effort to mask them. I do not hide them but gorge myself on them, showing the swan again and again how I would drown it, how if I were stronger and had the power of my jaws right now I would tear the wings from its body.

I am surprised and breathe in sharply as the swan drifts closer, its wings curled and its neck high and steady. It does not show any fear and I think that maybe it cannot understand, cannot interpret the thoughts I want it to see. But I am wrong, because I look into its eyes and when I do I see that not only has it seen everything, it understands what I have only just understood – that I show these things as a last act before my submission, before I plead with it to show me the way out of the cave as it did the fox.

We pause, our minds blank before the other. Perhaps it will ask me to return with food in exchange for the passage out. To prompt it I show the swan the image of the fox dropping food into the water, except this is a fox with a larger and greyer head, a single eye burning with aversion. The swan tilts its head again and in the muted flash of its eye I see that it doesn't seek this, it does not want me to feed it. Instead I feel in me the desire for my home, for the forest that is as much a part of me as I am of it and I realise that it is the swan that puts this seed in me and makes this desire a desperate and painful yearning, a lust stronger than any I have had for blood. It offers me my home. It offers me the thing I want more than anything, and then in its eyes there is something else – we are in among the trees and the snow with the sounds around us, but the trees are moving alongside me very slowly, and the snow is rising instead of falling. I am not moving any more but lying, looking up and watching the snow as it comes towards me, rising into it to become weightless.

The bird's perception shocks me. Does it see so clearly that I am dying? I know that I am near to death but to see it reflected in another's eyes is a new and horrifying event. I have looked at many and seen their death surround them – now before me something looks at me and sees the same. What a terrible thing to have something look at you this way!

And not only does it see my death, imminent and inescapable, I see that it understands what it is to have it follow you so, inevitable as the clouds beneath the moon. In its mind its thoughts of this are so complete that I am compelled – forced to enquire how it can know of this, asking it as if it were a brother of my kind. In the instant that it takes for my eye to flash over its request I realise with a sudden swallow that this also is wrong – it being the first time I have asked the thoughts of prey that have not been part of the hushed exchanges before its death. I expect shame to follow my question because of this and it is there, reminding me how weak I have become, taunting me with memories of what I was less than a whole day ago. But it is not so much that I must look away from the animal below me; I find that I can hold its gaze, and stand, and ignore the urge to dive through the rock onto the ledge outside and pitch myself off the cliff.

The swan takes me into its mind and I see through its eyes – I see the light of day on the roof of the cave suddenly wavering and then blocked, the fox appearing at the ledge and staring down at it as I do now. Then a second shape appears beside the fox, hazed and irregular until the light strengthens and I see that it is another fox and they stand shoulder to shoulder, two pairs of eyes and ears intent on the thing that looks up at them. I think that maybe the swan is confused, but then I remember the red shape the young fox had watched with fear climbing up the cliff face after the fallen bird. There must be two of them together – his mate perhaps. Why would they return to this stinking cave, to feed this tattered and unworthy prize, a prize they cannot kill and eat without becoming trapped within the cave themselves? I want to look away from the swan's thoughts because I think that this must be a deception – there must be a danger to me here, like a metal trap deep beneath twigs and dirt – but the swan holds my gaze and suddenly I feel fear as it does – an awful fear as it looks up at the foxes, and one that is felt constantly, waiting daily for the small predators to arrive, thinking each time that the moment it sees the light being blocked it will be the moment of its death.

Yes, the swan knows what it is to have death follow you. It must wish for death, living like this. Now it has moved closer. It is near enough that if I wanted I could easily swamp it with a quick jump forwards. Its neck is extended, its head held high, yet the water is far enough below that at full stretch its beak could not touch the lip of the rock on which I stand. In its eyes there is an eagerness: it is staring at me with a hunger not of the stomach but of the will – in the way it looks at me there is the vile, desperate shine of its hope and I realise with contempt and dawning horror that it sees me fallen and brought low by this injury and my weakness. It does not see me as the thing that has come to kill it, to end the misery of its constant fear of death. It sees me no longer as wolf, no longer as the killer and taker of life, but as the thing that will save it – that will release it from this cave!

All I can do is glare back at the swan, hot shame running through me that it could look at me this way. I back away from the edge, still holding the bird's gaze; it does not flinch or show fear at the anger it must see coursing through me. And though I am in this cave with its ceiling at my back, when I close my eye and block out the swan's expectant gleaming I can feel myself taken back to the forest, slowly sensing the wonderful softness of the earth beneath my paws, the smell of damp earth, the sound of birds singing and the lick of a warmer wind. It is autumn, and I do not know what it is that I am recalling until I see a hole beneath a tree in the deep brown ground – an old disused den, one that had long been deserted but that I was led to by the scent of another wolf.

I remember how I approached the den carefully, hearing the

sounds of laboured breathing, not seeing anything in the darkness of the den, and had stopped to sniff the ground again when, looking up, there was an old grey head deep in the entrance – a wolf with half an ear on one side, marks from many hunts or fights all over his long, thin snout. He was not standing but had merely raised his head from lying to see me, his whole body moving as he tried to suck the air in and push it back out. I watched as he took his last breath, listened to it whistle into a shallow chest, not understanding if he was injured, or maybe poisoned – and he must have seen the question in me because when he exhaled in his pale and misted eyes there was a sudden clarity. I saw the last, failing days of his life, how he had wandered a long time without eating, no longer able to hunt and so weak that he had limped among the beasts, none of them running or frightened and only a few turning their great heads half-curiously as he passed.

I think with shock that I have become like this – the walking dead, the hunter no longer able to hunt and waiting for slow starvation in front of the mocking eyes of former prey. Why else would the swan look at me the way it does? If I really am so weak then I may as well return to the cliff face outside and slip from its edge as if pushed. But I know, still, that that is a weakness too far and if there is the chance that I can return to my home I must take it, no matter how small and how low the path takes me.

I am still stood with my eye shut and when it opens into the dankness of the cave I expect my heart to drop and my new resolve to melt away into the stench and gloom. But it is the opposite. When I see it all – when I see the ragged swan below me, the low ceiling of rock and the black water that the bird, ridiculous in its prideful curve of neck, floats on I know that I will neither remain here nor leap to the ground behind me.

Stepping forwards until my head is over the water and I can feel the sharp edge of rock under my paw, I stare down at the bird, for a moment not knowing what to do, my eye blank like the swan's. Then the forest itself sends something piercing through me, as if it could somehow raise its head and scream into the air so that only I could hear it, this screaming suddenly filling me with thoughts and memories of my home, bright in their cleanliness of air and snow-covered ground and so vivid that I could not hide them from another if I wanted to. These thoughts and my lust for them must flow from me in a torrent because the swan moves backwards on the water as it sees them, as if their force and number is like a wind pushing out from me. I am opening my mind completely and I think that in desperation I must look ridiculous to the swan, shrieking as I am like a pup or a calf for the thing that I want. But beneath this flow that has pushed the bird back on the water there is another one where I am begging it constantly to show me the way out, like the current of colder water at the bottom of a stream, and it sees this and moves closer, closer than it has ever been, and I realise without joy what a fine, large animal it is and how, truly, it would have kept me fed for days.

Now in its eyes an image is forming. It is hazy and I lean even further over the water to get closer to it, blood from my head dripping again into the pool. The image is dark and I think that the swan does not know what it is trying to show me until I feel something beneath my jaw – the hard bite of rock – while over my head runs the faintest trickle of fresh air. It is the swan making me feel this and I think that these must be things it can sense but cannot see – perhaps even the exit to the cave.

This must be what it is showing me! Its neck does not reach

the ledge where I stand, so if it cannot itself escape, maybe it can just stretch up and get its beak on the lip of the route out. How it must have spent days at this place, gouging its head at the rock and trying to pull itself up, knowing that freedom was there above it and taunted by the smells coming from outside! I twitch with excitement at the prospect and the swan sees this and responds by showing me the fox again – a fox that shimmers and smears into a larger frame that could be my own. Again I see how it positions the fox and then I am down within it, the swan, floating on the water and feeling the rush of air as the fox powers itself up onto this other ledge.

But I am confused why it thinks that I will stand meekly and let myself be guided to make this jump. Perhaps this is its deception. Because if there is a ledge and the fox uses it almost daily then I will simply find it and leave. But even as I think this – a hope that the escape will be easy trying to form in me – I know there is doubt pulling it down like ivy an old tree. I look around the cave and my hopes of plunging in the water, killing the bird quickly and leaving by this other route plummet – they dissolve into the darkness that seems to fall at the back of the cave like a sheet of stone. Suddenly everything is clear, and I look back at the swan and see in it a hint of victory, because it knows that I understand that this exit route, this tunnel to which the fox jumps, is so shrouded in darkness that it is a leap made in complete blindness, impossible without the help of the bird.

I understand that I am powerless and it knows that I understand. Its eyes become blank, but in them it makes me see what it wants in return for this guidance: a flashing vision, as if it is afraid to reveal it, of my neck lowered prone in the darkness around which the swan's own grey flame-like neck is wrapped tight like a snake while I step slowly backwards, hauling it free from the pool up into the tunnel. It wants me to save it! It sees me with my crippled jaw and thinks because I am weak I will now help another also weak! Perhaps it dares to ask because it can see that I am dying. And it is also dying, I realise – not from injury or starvation but by dint of the foxes who slowly kill it each time they pass through: cunning to their nature, they must be keeping the swan alive until they have learnt the route by feel alone, each time getting a step closer to this, and the swan must know that one day they will not need its help to escape – one day they will come with empty jaws and the swan will know that it is breathing its last air. The foxes – they will kill, they will gorge themselves on its flesh and then pick their way out through the darkness unaided.

The swan is looking up at me, hoping to suckle agreement from my mind. Well – I may be weakened but it is far weaker than I – let it believe that I will help it! It sickens me – how can it hope that it might change my nature so completely that I would help it from this cave – but I must play along, become the thing it wants me to be. After all, it must first show me the way out. I only have to bear the shame of its kinship long enough to get me to the tunnel in the blackness back there, which even as I look to now strikes me as something solid. It must show me the way out first before I could possibly help it, so what is there to fear? All that I am afraid of is doing something I do not want to do. I realise this and feel, strength returning to me as the opportunity to deceive it, to flex my power over it, becomes solid – something my mind can bite at – and so I let my eye drop to the water and flick again to the swan, consent in its glimmer, anger and my will behind it like the heat of an ember.

The swan doesn't move for a moment and I watch it carefully to see if it knows my deceit. But then it is so filled with sudden hope that I do not worry and feel contempt rise into my shoulders, watching its eyes become bright in the gloom, like wet black stones, its head on its grazed neck wavering expectantly. Joy and excitement leak out from it like a scent, the painful tension of something being so close that it has wanted very much – something it thought it would never see and that has made the large curled feathers of its wings tremble with anticipation. I stand and look down at this bird with its greyed, dirt-streaked body and suddenly I am envious of its hope, of the way its tattered feathers quiver with it – its chance to live. How hateful it is to see another's prospect when you yourself have none!

I try to think of the satisfaction I will have when I leave it here, feeling my thoughts licking around the edges of its abandonment like my tongue would the haunch of something, yet even this small pleasure I cannot indulge for fear of the swan seeing it running through me. Instead I show my consent to help it again and the swan slips back on the water, making a space of shining black surface in front of it, an invitation to enter. Hesitantly I shift my weight to my front paws and the edge of the rock ledge, sniffing involuntarily at the water below, repelled by the rich smell of stagnancy and decay that lies above it. I have never been fond of water though I know I can swim powerfully, but to jump into this oily darkness is something else. The swan remains stationed in the middle of the pool, watching me fixedly, its eyes and posture of one intent to pull me forwards and begging me to jump – it seems to be willing and pleading with all of itself that I might step forwards from the rock lying so solidly beneath my paws.

I move backwards slightly and lower into a crouch, preparing to jump. Suddenly I think it is a trap – the swan will surely deceive me and I will be drowned in that horrible water – perhaps it will even try to smother me itself or beat at me with its wings. But I know that this is just my fear of what is ahead, as what I saw in the swan's eyes – the hope of freedom it now holds to – could not possibly be anything other than the truth. I searched for deception in that gaze because then its prospect would have been a lie, and I would not have to look at it and hate it. There was none and I only hesitate to delay what is to follow.

So I crouch lower into my hind legs and lower still, hearing my heart clicking, and then I spring forwards to fall downwards through the air, a space too brief before I hit the water, my legs splayed and my head held high and away from the liquid that is quickly around my neck and over my back – stinking and cold and thick – more like mud than water. Then I am struggling, swimming forwards without knowing where to go, turning sharply in the water in search of the floating bird, all the while feeling the strength of my muscles slipping away, the water sucking at my paddling limbs, each stroke an effort against it. I make another sharp turn and suddenly the bird is beside me; effortlessly it glides in front and seeing its grey shape I follow it, struggling to keep within the ripples it makes as it swims.

The swan leads me further into the cave, the light fading as we move until I can only just make out its shape in front of me. Then the light fades completely and I am lost – I can no longer see the swan and can neither smell nor hear its movement. But then I feel a pressure at my side, not hard like rock but soft and with the warmth of living flesh, and as I swim forwards it pushes against me, or drifts away so that with rising panic I must turn towards it to seek its heat in the darkness.

I swim with the swan guiding me for what seems too long

a time – surely the cave cannot be this large! The strength has left my legs completely. The water is up to my eye and completely over my back and shoulders and I raise my snout up as if howling to get at the air above the surface. I seem not to be moving, only kicking so that I do not sink, and I have already thought it impossible that I could kick another stroke when my claws scratch on something hard and solid in the water before me. I kick and clamber forwards, feeling the rock slope upwards beneath the water – yet by careful wading back and forth finding that at no point does the smooth stone break the surface. Instead it lies submerged so that at its peak my paws are still completely covered by the cloying wetness. But at last I stand on something like land and do not have to fight against the thickness of the water. I stand motionless and suck at the air shallowly, my head a haze of lightness and mild pain, my limbs and neck numb shadows of a former movement.

To my side I hear the sound of rippling water, then a louder splash: the bird, I realise, coming towards me invisibly in the darkness. I feel the sudden pressure of its beak against my leg, pushing with firm and forceful movements – unpleasant quick stabs that anger me and make me wish that I could strike out and snap the neck that dares to touch me. I no longer have the power to do this and even if I did I'm not sure that I would – the brief moment of satisfaction it would bring would not make up for the slow death in this cave – and so I drop my head and let myself be pecked at and pushed. Even though it is completely black I close my eye and submit, and while there is shame there, there is also relief – for a moment I am no longer myself – I have none of the power and none of the hungers or desires that go with it. I am nothing and feel as if my bones are hollow like a bird's.

Then the guidance stops. I hear a rustle and the soft sound of water slightly moved and I am left standing alone, facing a black wall of darkness, my submerged paws chilled to the bone. The swan has moved away and I can hear it breathing at my side. Now it hisses – a sharp sound that circles in the echoing confines of stone, a noise made part in demand and part in request, willing me to leap forwards – the same terrible hiss that it would utter if I had its youngster in my jaws.

I raise my head and sniff at the blackness ahead, searching for the scent of fresh air that might reveal the opening of a tunnel to the outside – although either the stench of the water is too overpowering or there is none because I can smell nothing of the clean winter beyond. Again I hear the swan hiss at my side. Now it is not so terrible – more the hiss of something desperate and weak than something that could break you with a swipe of its wing. I do not want to follow its command; I don't want to leap blindly into a black space or be made to leap by anything other than myself, and for a moment I feel stubbornness adding to the ice around my paws, wondering what taste of satisfaction I might have if I were to just stand here, letting the swan suck in and hiss out this foul air in frustration. There would be no satisfaction, though, being stood here with my feet in water. Feeling something settle inside me, I lower my body so that my legs are taut like saplings, and thinking of nothing but my home leap forwards into the darkness with all the power I have remaining. The ground gone from my feet I steel myself for the impact of stone or water, passing through the air for an unbearably long time, knowing that at any instant something hard and unknown will strike out of the black to hit me. Then it does and I am surprised – suddenly there is rock beneath my body, and although I am unbalanced and fall it feels no worse than tripping on earth.

Slowly I get to my feet, a hind paw slipping into air before I pull it back in – that must be the drop into the pool behind me. I am able to stand and as I raise my head, even in the dark I sense that there is more space above, and what is that? There is the faintest trickle of air coming from the outside – a weak scent but with direction, a trail for me to follow – and stepping away from the awful cave I feel the first joy of freedom trickle through me. And although I know it is an illusion it feels like the first real joy I have ever truly had, like sunshine, like the night sky and the smell of fresh snow.

I have taken only a few steps forwards when I hear the sound behind me. First there is the splashing of water, then the sound of something beating slowly but getting faster and faster until it sounds like a frenzy, air and water beaten into a whirling mass of noise as if the ground of the forest had turned into water and all the trees were collapsing into it at the same time. And then above this horrible thrashing I think I hear wailing, a desperate scream that is more like a hiss, a spitting out of air in fury and complete desolation – an awful sound of suffering that strikes me to the spot as if I am made of ice.

I have stopped but the sound continues behind me. I hear

the swan's wings beating against the stone wall below the tunnel's entrance, its feet gouging at the water, trying to push it upwards and out – the sharp sound of its beak snapping against the rock, trying to find purchase as if it might haul itself up with its thin weak neck. I turn my head and the sounds begin to calm – the thrashing wings lessen as the swan tires, the sound of its beak clacking against the rock becoming less frequent, and I imagine it throwing its head forwards and upwards with less effort, with less hope. Yet as its struggles become quiet, above the lapping the disturbed water makes against the side of the pool rises a harsh and rasping sound, a sound as if something is breathing yet suffocating – the sounds I realise to be the swan exhaustedly gasping at the stench-filled air of its prison. I listen to its pitiful breaths, breaths taken only because its body and lungs must be screaming from the effort, breaths not to keep it alive but to continue its awful suffering, sucked inwards and hissed out mechanically and with no real desire for life – I listen to these echoing breaths and my step falters.

How I would love to turn and crush the life from the neck of that bird!

Here I stand with this rock beneath me, half-turned, with escape and freedom at my side, yet behind me a creature is suffering as all the others have – a creature I have failed – a creature I am unable to kill and must leave floundering in its desperation. Standing here listening to its easing breaths I find that I pity the swan. But then I have pitied them all their horrible suffering, those that I have ripped and brought down and eaten or just left lying slumped on the ground for the crows and insects. I pity them all that they are weak! That they are weak, flawed and forced to run over the earth in terror of their own disadvantage while I exist, stronger and faster, quicker in mind, and to satisfy my hunger must fly through from the shadows at them with burning eyes and be their killer. And though I have always known what it is to pity – though I have always run and snarled and torn flesh with its bitter taste in my mouth it is only now that I am no longer strong that it makes me hesitate, that it stops my muscles and separates them from the points of my teeth. Now I too am weak like they are. Wounded, I have been brought low to roam among them in fear of death and suffering, and where before I knew pity, now that I am weak I can feel it.

Silently I turn and make my way back towards the pool. As I approach I can hear the swan's breaths echoing in the cave and again the sound of the water lapping at the stone sides of the pool. I think that the bird must have lost all hope, because if it had been listening it would have heard the small scraping my paws make and that I try to mask with careful steps – or perhaps it hears yet does not believe or does not understand why I should return. I creep back towards it, still with stealth because I am afraid – I fear the terrible futile sound of a renewed struggle for its freedom – and if there is the chance that I could turn again and vanish without being noticed I will not give myself away by making noise. Perhaps even I would not be able to leave hearing that sound again – the sound of a struggle I can't end with death as I would dearly like, instead a suffering I must end through help: an act that I dread but that holds me here against my nature.

I am close enough to know that a further step could pitch me back over into the water, so I creep forwards hesitantly, searching for the lip of the rock, more pawing than stepping. I can smell the swan and hear its whistling gasps not far off in the darkness. These breaths – I hate every one of them and every part of their sound! In the darkness there is only the swan's scent and the sound of its breathing, but these sounds fill my mind the way snow will drop and fill a nook in a tree: I see in a shimmering confusion how the bird might have been and how it really is – and also what I was and what I have become. Each breath I hear is like a blow or something biting at me, and while my body is still, something within me is crushed smaller and smaller until it is like stone.

Suddenly its breaths stop and there is the deep silence of two natural enemies listening for the other: a still, solid silence where the smallest sound becomes the clearest movement. I make no signal for the swan. I cling to the hope that I might remain undetected, like a young deer sitting as still as stone within high grass. But the blood leaking slowly from my head and pooling in my jaw spills from my mouth to drip in the water below, a sound the swan must sense as different from the other quiet drippings for its breathing has begun again and I can hear it moving towards me, its rasping breaths becoming closer, then the sound of water rippling beneath me.

To turn away now would start the sound of it struggling against the rock and the water – a sound that tries to tear my muscles from my bones – something I do not think I can hear again without being able to bring about its end. But I cannot bring myself to help this creature – I cannot bring myself to lower my head and feel the clinging grasp of its snake-like neck. It is not my nature – it is not our nature, neither the bird's nor mine, that we find ourselves locked together like this: the swan expecting to be saved and me hesitating to walk away from it. On any of the other days of my life I would have left it by now. Only at this moment do I hesitate, only at this very moment and it must be because I am wounded – the blood that runs off my chin and neck tries to take with it what I am and have been and deaden the feeling of what it is beneath my feet. But I feel it now – I feel the cold stone underneath my claws, and raising my back and head I step backwards away from the pool, quickly and without stealth, slowly scraping my claws so that I feel every ridge in the smoothness of the rock and so that the swan will clearly hear me leaving.

I turn and begin to pad away down the tunnel, expecting at any moment to hear the sound of its frayed wings beating at the air, but no sound comes. There is only silence behind me – a silence I realise to be that of total resignation to further horror, an acceptance of certain and close death. This silence is worse to me than the sound of its struggle, and even its desperate breaths, because in it I know that it must see all that has passed and all the torment that is to come. It is the silence of comprehension – like the final terror in the hare's eye in the instant its body becomes limp in consent, the moment to me most distasteful of all, the moment they give up and know they must be slain and I must kill them quickly to end the horror of it all, the weakness of sympathy I have for them swathed in sharply flashing teeth and crushing jaw. And now I exist in this moment – a moment that should last an instant but instead stretches before me without end – and if I were to leave and try to walk home my weakened legs would be further weighted by the shame and sheer, crushing sadness of abandoning suffering without delivering its end – a new pain I cannot endure and one that fires me to rage.

I turn sharply and step towards the scent of water. I reach the edge of rock and listen for the bird's presence, wondering if it may have swum back towards the other end of the cave – then I hear its muted, tired breaths coming from somewhere near and below. Perhaps it thinks that I have come back to taunt it, as it seems to make no movement in the darkness, and in my anger I omit a low and wavering growl, part call, part threat – a snarl that gurgles the blood in my mouth into a thick foam to seep between my teeth. I hear movement in the water coming closer towards me, a slow deliberate paddling that seems designed to tell me clearly of the swan's approach, a sound that seems to lack all guile and only holds a horrible whispering intent. Now I feel movement at my paws, the bird's beak tentatively searching for me in the darkness – an exploration made so hesitantly that I think I can sense its sheer disbelief, or is it that I am just flooded with it myself?

Slowly I lower my wounded head, steeling myself for the strength of the swan's scent and the soft awful touch of its neck, which rises suddenly from the black to cling to mine and wrap itself around me, a contact that at first I think I cannot stand and must shake off with violence, yet in its startling strength almost a comfort and not the cold, limp grasp I had expected. I step slowly backwards and feel the weight of the bird as I haul it upwards – a weight that at first seems too heavy and then becomes surprisingly light – an act that is hardly an effort even in my weakened state and one that is soon completed, the swan free from the pool and standing on the stone before me as I shrug off its neck and twirl around, stepping blindly down along the tunnel, stumbling on the uneven surface, smearing myself against its unseen walls as I run away outwards and away from the cave.

The tunnel is long and I am often tripped by its hidden edges, but with the scent of fresh air becoming stronger I move forwards without caution or care for the injuries that scrape and cut my legs, or even the shattering pain that strikes my head when I stumble, because I get up quickly and move forwards, pushed by what is behind me, pulled up and further down the tunnel by what blood remains inside my chest. At first when the black before me seems to become a shade of grey I think that I deceive myself, but then my eye can suddenly make out shapes in the darkness, the tunnel stretching before me with a strange clarity while whispers of cold, clean air flow over me in a glorious freshness. Another turn and suddenly I see the bright shocking light of day framed in the round opening of the tunnel's exit, and seeing it I am struck with relief at my release from the stench and intimacy of the cave, though it is a joy immediately dulled by the realisation that I am dangerously and irreversibly weakened and will not last long to savour it.

But along with the freshness of the winter air is a scent that, though unexpected, is of little surprise. In the light ahead appear two vague shapes, unclear in the dazzle of sudden brightness, but matched with their distinctive smell instantly recognisable for the small, cunning predators that they are. I approach slowly and stand before the two red foxes – one the young male that led me here, the other an older female – not his mate as I had thought but his mother. The young one is afraid, his eyes watch me fearfully and his legs tremble and quiver as if cold from the wind that ripples his fur. But he is not cold, he is just afraid, unlike his mother who stands peacefully, her delicate head held high, the tips of her small teeth exposed beneath her thin black lips and her eyes – her green eyes as cold as stone and staring at me with vicious expectancy. In her glance is all the deadliness of female savagery, the fierceness that loves and protects her young above all else – the will and strength that at its centre is nothing but an untouchable coldness – a thing blind and deaf to anything else, to any other call or signal.

While the foxes bar my way ahead I hear the faintest sound

of something behind me – a sound so small that either the foxes do not hear, as they are standing where the wind blows noisily into the opening, or in cunning make no indication that they have heard what must and can only be the swan, who must still be out of sight, concealed behind the hidden bend in the tunnel. I stand and look at the two red shapes in front of me who still make no move apart from the youngster's trembling, and suddenly I am filled with grudging admiration for their guile – the cleverness that has brought them here in the hope of a meal and that they wait for patiently in ambush – a cunning I would myself employ had I my strength and my wits rather than this sleepy weakness that slithers around my head and body.

How I must look to them, standing here, my own blood running down to my paws. I know now that I will not be able to return home, that my body only has the strength for one more disappearance into my will. I can feel that I am dying and am almost dead – I can feel it and nothing now could carry me back to the forest. But I will not be killed by man! I will not be killed by his weapon alone, and with this belief I feel the ground beneath me and all my strength launching me forwards towards the young fox, a movement so quick and powerful that he is helpless to react and is again knocked into the snow. I turn weakly towards the vixen but already she is on me and I can feel her teeth against my throat, the sharpness of their points the only feeling in my body as the breath is choked from my lungs and the last of my blood leaks from my head.

And as a coldness beyond the snow and ice of winter begins to freeze me – a tiredness further than exhaustion starting to close my eye – I think of the swan, and wonder at the cloud I see, and how sometimes clouds can look like living things.

ACKNOWLEDGEMENTS

I would like to acknowledge Barry Lopez for his influential book *Of Wolves and Men*, which I read as a child, but have never forgotten.